Wolf of Ash

Rejected Shifter Series, Volume 1

Amelia Shaw

Published by Tamsin Baker, 2021.

This is a work of fiction. Similarities to real people, places, or events are entirely coincidental.

WOLF OF ASH

First edition. October 29, 2021.

Copyright © 2021 Amelia Shaw.

Written by Amelia Shaw.

Chapter 1

Talia

In six days, I was marrying the next Alpha of the Northwood pack. Maddox Brady. My fated mate.

Lights flashed around me and the room spun with the beat of the heavy techno music the DJ was playing. I didn't dare get up from the stool where I teetered, lest I fall flat on my face. Yet, despite my intoxication, the simple fact was, I'd never been happier. I loved Maddox and couldn't wait to marry him.

"Another round of tequila shots!" I called to the bartender, though I wasn't sure he'd bring them. He'd said something about cutting us off earlier, but surely he'd been joking?

"You can't handle another round, Talia," said Nyssa, my best friend.

I leaned forward on my stool and straightened my pink and white sash. We all had them. Mine read, 'Bride-to-be'.

"This is my last night as a single lady!" I sang the words, amazed at how loud I could be when the music thumped around me like a drum in my ear. "Gotta make every minute count."

Nyssa laughed. "The mating ceremony's not for another week, Talia. You've still got time."

"Here, I got you another one," Celia whispered, handing me a small glass of clear liquor. My other best friend had come through for me.

I took the drink, my hand wobbling as I brought it to my lips. I snorted, then tipped my head back, throwing the shot down my throat.

"Wow." I grimaced at the burn, and handed Celia back the glass. Then I took a deep breath and focused on the warm feeling of the alcohol spreading through my veins.

Oh, yeah. That has to be the last one. Or I'll never make it home.

Thank goodness the wedding was next week and not tomorrow.

Then again, if it *was* tomorrow, I would never have gotten this smashed.

"Are you excited for the wedding night?" Nyssa asked me, wiggling her eyebrows up and down.

Celia snickered, while I rolled my eyes. They all knew I couldn't wait to finally consummate my relationship with Maddox.

My fated mate.

My true love.

The future Alpha of our pack.

"Of course, she is!" Celia answered for me.

Celia was my oldest friend. We'd known each other practically from the day we'd been born. Her mom and mine were friends from way back, and we'd been raised together as more sisters, than anything else.

Celia turned to me with an eyebrow raised. She was by far the most sober of us. "You never told us what the real reason was."

I leaned forward on the bar stool, careful not to crush the peanuts lying on the surface of the bar top, then squinted at my friend. "For what?"

Celia glared at me. "For waiting this long to have sex with him!"

I gasped at her forwardness, then put a hand over my mouth and giggled.

I shook my head, not wanting to answer.

She jabbed me in the arm with her finger and I swayed on my seat. "Whoa..."

"Come on, Talia! You can tell us!"

Nyssa nodded. "Yeah. I want to know why, too."

I hefted my top for the tenth time, trying to cover up the ridiculous amount of cleavage this outfit showed off to the room, and shrugged.

"We just... decided to wait."

I didn't want to admit it hadn't been my decision. Maddox had been adamant though. We needed to get married first.

Celia pulled another stool over to the bar and huddled closer so she could hear me better. The music was loud, and the people dancing and drinking on this warm summer night were even louder.

I closed my eyes, enjoying the heat of the room and the warmth in my blood. As the next Alpha's mate, I was watched constantly when we were at home. In the pack. In town. At formal gatherings.

I tried to be as perfect as possible. For Maddox. For the current Alpha of the Northwood pack. And also for my dad.

But tonight was my bachelorette party. I could finally let down my hair and not worry about anyone else and what they might think of me.

The steady beat and thump of one of my favorite songs came through the speakers. I jumped to my unsteady feet, wobbling on the tiny heels Nyssa had made me wear.

"Let's dance!"

I pulled my two best friends to the dance floor. They were my entire bridal party and all I needed. I began to sway and twerk and giggle away.

This wasn't my last night of freedom, of course. But it was one of my last nights as a single woman. Soon I would be a mate, a wife, and the future Alpha's mate, with all the responsibilities that came with that position.

And I couldn't wait.

"Is Maddox doing his bachelor party tonight too?" Celia asked, dancing forward to whisper the question into my ear.

I twirled toward her. "Doesn't matter, 'cos I'm here with you!"

I grabbed her hands and spun around, almost falling on my ass, but managing to stay on my feet.

Just.

We laughed and danced, and drank more, thanks to Celia.

Close to dawn, we all caught a cab back to the pack, then staggered into the house I shared with my father.

"Your dad doesn't mind if we stay over?" Celia asked, throwing her dress to the floor and crawling into my bed with her underwear still in place.

I dragged the curtains shut, blocking out the rising sun. "Course not. You guys are family."

The girls smiled as they settled on either side of the bed.

I took a drunken moment to appreciate how lucky I was to have these two in my life. As an only child, these girls were the closest thing I had to sisters.

I stripped off my own clothes, relieved when my short skirt and too-obvious top were in a pile on the floor. I enjoyed being pretty like every other girl, but boobs and legs on show everywhere was not usually my style.

"The house is really quiet. So is the rest of the town," Celia whispered, her eyes closing as she nestled into the pillow she'd landed on.

I crawled onto the king-sized bed and slid under the covers between my friends.

"Dad's out. He said there was some pack business thing they had to do today."

Nyssa huffed out a laugh as she rolled over. "You're the future Alpha's mate and you still don't get told anything, huh?"

"Yeah..." I lied, and closed my eyes.

I knew where they'd all gone, which was probably half the reason I'd drunk so much tonight. But we'd gotten on the water around two a.m., and now that I was well on the way to sober thanks to my wolf metabolism, the anxiety had set back in.

Maddox, my dad, and the rest of the men in our pack had planned an attack today. On a neighboring pack they considered a major threat.

The Long Claw Pack. Their Alpha was legendary for his strength, as was his son, Galen. Though I hadn't met either of them.

Personally, I hated the wars the wolves fought amongst themselves. It didn't make sense to me when we had so many other natural enemies. We all had our own territories, so why wolves constantly fought for more power, was beyond me.

And I hated the fact that the men I loved put themselves in danger like this.

I rolled onto my side and let exhaustion sweep me away. I tried not to dream about the dangers my family were in. After all, my dad and Maddox were my whole world.

GALEN

My eyes sprung open at the sound of running footsteps thumping through my dad's house.

The door to my bedroom flung open and I sat bolt upright in bed.

"We're being raided." One of my betas, Tommy, pushed the door wide. "It's those fuckers from the Northwood Pack. They're here."

I jumped out of bed and rapidly pulled on some old jeans. One of the fifty pairs I kept for moments like this: when I knew I was going to shift, and probably destroy the clothing in a split second.

"Go," I told Tommy. "I'll be there straight away."

Tommy ran out the door again.

I didn't bother with a sweatshirt. This was going to be a fight, not a conversation. I didn't need to dress properly.

I chased after Tommy, ducking into my dad's room on the way, where he lay in his bed, fast asleep and as pale as the sheets he lay on. He had a light sheen of sweat decorating his brow.

Dad hadn't been well for months, so there was no way I was waking him now. If he knew they'd come, he'd want to join the fight, and in his current state, it was highly unlikely he'd survive. He could barely stand, let alone shift and defend our territory against a bunch of strong wolves.

I wasn't ready to be Alpha of my dad's Long Claw Pack. Not yet.

And I wasn't ready to live in a world without my dad in it.

"Galen!" Tommy hissed from the front door. "Come on!"

I hightailed it out of my dad's room and reached the front door. "What do we know?"

"The Northwood Pack is about to attack. Our scouts have seen them coming through the woods."

"How many are there?" I asked, already mentally preparing for the fight we were about to have.

The neighboring pack had always hated our borders, though I wasn't sure why. There was bad blood from way back before I was born and no one had ever mentioned what happened back then.

But why attack? And why now?

Had they heard my father was dying and our pack would need to fight without our Alpha? That was the most likely explanation for this timing.

Assholes.

They thought we were weak without my dad. We'd just have to prove them wrong.

"At least thirty strong," Tommy said. "Maybe more."

I nodded once. They'd brought most of their pack. The men anyway.

I hope their Alpha is with them. I'd love to take him out. Or his pussy of a son. Maddox.

"Let's go."

I was next in line to my father, born from a long line of Alphas. I could lead our men in this fight. And, victorious, or not, I would never abandon them.

Tommy and I ran through the town, waking up our fellow pack mates and shouting out orders. "Lock the doors. Make sure your families remain safe."

All our women were strong fighters if need be, but it was their job to protect our children if something happened to the men.

It was our role to protect them, so that hopefully they'd never have to fight to save their babies.

I called to my Betas. "Let's get to the forest edge."

Our town was built well and was only vulnerable from two sides.

I had at least forty men, so I could afford to divide our forces.

"Split up! You five go to the east." It was unlikely the neighboring pack would attack that way. Their lands lay to the south. But I didn't want to leave any of our borders unmanned, just in case. "The rest of you follow me."

We ran to the south side, where the forest butted up against the town. My heart pounded like a war drum in my chest. Adrenaline zinged along my veins.

The only question in my mind was whether I needed to shift straight away, or later. We didn't carry weapons, but my claws were razor sharp, as were my teeth.

"There!" someone cried, and I squinted into the darkness of the forest.

The sun was only beginning to lift its head. Whisps of red and orange hues rose about the horizon, lighting up the blackened sky.

Deep in the forest, wolves stalked toward us. They'd already shifted, their beady yellow eyes standing out against the darkness around them.

Well, I'm not getting caught out with my fragile human body. They're clearly not here to talk. That's for damn certain.

I let go of my humanity. My wolf rose inside me, growling loudly as it took over.

I dropped to the ground onto all fours. My whole body vibrated as my skin sprouted fur, and I transformed into the huge beast of my forefathers.

My black wolf form.

And then it was on.

They charged, and every man around me shifted. The dawn filled with the snarls of the wolves from two packs—mine, and theirs.

There was no warm-up, no formalities, as the neighboring pack ran out of the woods toward us. This was going to be a fight to the death, and I damn sure wasn't going down today. Not on my land. Not on my father's death watch.

I flew at the nearest wolf rushing forward, my mouth open, teeth ready.

He snapped in my face, missing his mark as I twisted. I tore around the side of him, ripping my teeth through his fur and tasting blood on my tongue.

The wolf yelped and skittered sideways, before teaming up with another gray wolf near him and coming back for a second try.

They both faced me, their lips raised in matching snarls. I charged, aiming for the new wolf, and head butted him, then bared my teeth to the one I'd already injured.

He should have run when he had the chance.

This time I grabbed him around the throat, my ears burning with his whimper a moment before I tore out his throat. Blood gushed into my mouth.

His neck snapped as he fell to the ground, his head tilted at an odd angle, and I turned to growl at the other wolf.

They'd come onto my land, into our town, to what? Kill us all? Even the women and children?

Not today.

The other wolf started to back away, before lifting his head and howling. It was a high-pitched sound that set my fur on edge. He was calling for help.

I charged, my mouth open, and sunk my teeth around the wolf's neck and shook him. Hard.

Enough to warn, not kill. If he came at me again, I wouldn't give him a second chance.

He scrabbled into the dirt to get away from me, and I let him.

He whined as he backed away, toward the forest.

I backed up a few steps also, watching as their pack rejoined forces and grouped together near the forest's edge once more.

Where was their leader?

There. A large black wolf who met my eyes. He was still in challenge mode, but he was wavering. I could read the uncertainty in his expression.

I stepped over body after body of dead wolves to get back to the rest of my pack. The guys, my betas, were blood-smeared and panting, but looked mostly okay.

I stood at the head of the Long Claw Pack and growled at the intruders that had come from the Northwood. It was their call. Would they regroup and try again, or would they turn tail and retreat? We wouldn't chase them if they chose the latter.

The large black wolf howled once, and as one, the whole pack turned away. Their Alpha, the one in charge, had called an end to the fight.

Good decision.

I let myself begin to relax. They were leaving.

Then suddenly, a large gray wolf growled and broke away from the retreating group, running around their pack to head straight at me.

This lone wolf was trying to take me out? Seriously?

But he wasn't alone for long. As he ran, others followed, until he'd managed to pull several wolves away from the main pack. They were all coming toward me now.

I shook my head as I faced them.

Idiots.

They'd just lessened the numbers of their main group by ten, all the while bringing the party to me. Perfect.

I dug my feet into the dirt and launched at them.

Then the whole pack came at us. They'd obviously decided to join the second wave.

We fought hard, and I killed two more of their wolves before the other side called another retreat.

I stared after them as the remaining wolves ran for their lives through the woods, back the way they had come. In that second attack, they'd lost at least five more pack members, and I almost growled at the stupidity of it all.

I let go of my shifter, rising from my animal posture to stand on two feet again.

My naked skin was covered in sweat and my heart thumped loudly in my chest as the adrenaline took time to dissipate.

"Should we go after them?" Markus asked, having transformed back to human beside me. He was huffing and puffing from exertion.

Blood poured down his chest from a wound in his shoulder.

I shook my head. "We will avenge this attack, but not today. Right now, we patch up our injured, and burn the bodies of their fallen."

They'd gotten what they deserved, coming onto our land to try and kill us while we slept. They had twelve dead, if I counted correctly, and many others of them had been injured. A huge hit to any pack. They were weaker now. There would be no coming back until they regrouped, which gave me time to plan our attack.

I glanced around at my own pack members. Several injured, and two dead. There would be justice. Our pack would have its vengeance.

Chapter 2

Talia

My father limped into the house after I'd said goodbye to a still hungover Nyssa and Celia.

I'd barely slept all morning, worried about my father and Maddox and how they were going during their attack on the neighboring pack. But even so, I'd not expected them back so soon.

"Dad!" I ran out to greet him as he practically fell through the front door. "Let me help you."

I put my arm around his waist and partly carried him to the couch, where he dropped onto the cushions. He was bleeding from wounds in his leg and chest.

Not life-threatening, by the looks of them, but not pleasant. "I'll get the first aid kit."

"Thanks." He groaned as he hoisted his leg up onto the couch.

I grabbed a bottle of water and the box of supplies I kept on hand in the kitchen, then rushed back to my dad.

"What happened?" I asked, wincing at the blood gushing onto our couch. "That's gonna need stiches."

"Thanks, Talia," he said, lying back and getting comfortable on the cushions behind him.

I sighed and pulled up a stool. That meant I needed to do the stitches for him. Dad didn't really like going to the doctor in town. I'd done this before, but I still didn't like it.

I threaded the needle and flicked the lighter so I could burn the end to sterilize the metal. With a shifter's metabolism, infections were rare, but for the few seconds it took to do the extra step, I figured it couldn't hurt. I liked to be thorough.

"Can you tell me what happened, Dad?"

He sighed, a heavy, world-weary sigh. "I did something stupid."

My head flew up and I stared at him. "What do you mean?"

"I tried to go for the young Alpha."

I bent my head to the task, carefully, but firmly holding the torn flesh of my dad's leg together so I could slide the needle through.

"What was the mission, exactly?"

"To take out the old Alpha, and his son Galen, if we could."

"But why?"

Dad shrugged. "Pack politics aren't my thing, Taley, you know that. Let's talk about something else for a minute. You're about to get married. That's the most important think that can happen in your life."

I glanced up. "You really think so? The most important?"

Dad nodded solemnly, then winced as I continued to sew up his leg wound. The chest laceration would be next, but it wasn't bleeding as much. "Yes," he said. "Everything else is easy to fix if you make a mistake. Wrong house, wrong job. But choosing a mate... or having fate choose one for you... that is the biggest decision of your life. It shapes who you are, who your children will be, and how you live your life."

That was the most I'd heard my dad say in one go in a very long time.

"Is that how you felt about Mom?" I asked gently, concentrating on my stitching and not looking up at my dad.

He usually didn't like to talk about her, no matter how much I asked.

"Yes," he said simply.

I risked a glance at his face to see a soft smile playing at the edges of his lips.

"She was... incredible," he said with a sigh. "The most amazing woman I've ever known."

Hot tears gathered in my eyes and I blinked them away, trying to concentrate on my sewing task. "Why don't you ever talk about her?"

He groaned, shifting slightly in obvious discomfort. "I don't know... too painful, I guess."

I sniffed, trying my best to hide the emotions I was feeling and the tears that were still gathering, ready to flow.

I coughed to clear my throat and tied off the thread. I was done with my sewing.

"Because she died?"

I faced him squarely this time, and my dad stared straight at me. "Yeah."

"I know you never wanted to talk about it before, but how did she die, Dad?" Every time I'd brought up the topic, he changed the conversation, or flat out refused to talk about it.

"You almost done?" Dad asked, indicating his leg.

A punch of disappointment hit me in the chest. I was going to be left wondering again, it seemed.

"Ah, yeah. I might just wrap it up lightly. And the chest, too. Hang on."

I pressed gauze to the fresh stitches and wrapped tape around the leg wound, then spent a few minutes cleaning and taping the gash on his chest. It was shallow and didn't require stitches the way his leg had. For a human, this quick patch-up job wouldn't be adequate; nowhere near it. Neither would my stitching have been.

But my father wasn't human. He was a strong, huge, wolf shifter. And as far as I knew, my mother had been the same.

Not that I remembered her particularly well.

Once I was done, he lifted his leg and swung it off the side of the couch. He panted and cursed a little, but then smiled at me. "Thanks."

I nodded and made to get up from my stool.

Dad reached out for me and grabbed my arm. "Can you stay a bit? Sit with me."

He had never asked me to do such a thing before.

"Yeah, of course. Is there something you need to tell me?" My heart sickened. "Is Maddox okay? He came back from the fight, didn't he?"

I jumped to my feet and stared out the window, my stomach suddenly churning.

Several pack members stood around talking, but no one was coming this way. No one even seemed to be looking at our house.

That was a good sign.

"Maddox is fine." I relaxed slightly at his words. Then he added, "He didn't get too close to the front of the action." I couldn't help but notice the disgust in his voice when he said it.

Conflicting emotions rose in me. The instant desire to defend my mate, and the knowledge that dodging action in a fight was a cowardly act, in shifter terms.

It was a cowardly act, in any language.

"You know his dad doesn't let him do anything dangerous, when he can help it," I said, and swallowed hard against the acid that rose in my throat.

Our Alpha only had one son, like most shifters in our pack. One child. One son. And the Alpha made sure to keep his heir safe.

Other pack members thought that was the wrong thing to do. They believed that the only way to harden up a wolf shifter—especially a fighter and someone who would one day be a leader—was to throw him into the fray. Experience bred the best generals. But that wasn't my decision to make.

On a personal level, I was glad that Maddox was home, and he was safe. I'd never really had to worry about him in the past, which was probably why he hadn't been the first thing on my mind when Dad had come back injured.

"Anyway." Dad coughed hard. "About your question."

I moved closer. He had my full attention now. "You mean about Mom?"

He nodded. "There isn't a lot to tell, Taley. I wish I had some grand, amazing story to tell you, but she just… died. It was an accident."

I swallowed hard. I'd been eight years old when my mom died. Which meant I had some beautiful memories of her kindness, her hugs, and her voice, but not a lot of concrete things that would help me interpret what my dad was trying to say.

"What do you mean exactly by… it was an accident?"

My heart was pumping a little too fast in my chest. Did he mean that she'd fallen off a cliff while on a hike, or had he accidentally killed her while in a wolf-shifter rage or something? What?

"It was a car accident," Dad said quietly. "She was driving home from work in the city. She was a nurse. She'd picked up some late shifts to help pay the bills. I was…. out of work again. I just…"

He stopped to run a shaking hand through his hair. "She should never have been driving home that late. It was past midnight. Raining…"

My heart broke to hear the lump in his throat, the regret and pain he was pushing past to speak about what had happened.

He blamed himself? I reached over and grabbed his hand. "Things like that happen, Dad. It sucks, and I hate it. But it wasn't your fault."

It couldn't have been. He wasn't the rain. He wasn't the car. He wasn't even the one driving.

I shuddered at the thought of the guilt someone would feel to be driving a car, only to crash and kill their passengers. That load would be something that would truly break your heart. But Dad hadn't been there. He shouldn't blame himself.

When he raised his gaze to meet mine, there was so much love burning behind his eyes, it took my breath away.

He squeezed my hand tight. "You're the only reason I'm still here, my beautiful daughter."

I frowned and held tight to his hand, relishing in the rare show of affection from my father. "What do you mean, Dad?"

"I mean that I don't think I would have lived the past fifteen years without you." He smiled and reached over to cup my cheek with his other hand.

I covered his hand with mine. "You've been my whole world, Dad. Thank you... for everything."

I swallowed hard, forcing the emotional lump down.

We hadn't always gotten along, of course. Like most girls with their dads, especially during my teenage years when puberty kicked in, and I tried testing boundaries as all teens do. But he'd supported me, loved me, given me a home, and kept me safe.

In this world, I couldn't ask for more.

There was a long, drawn-out moment, where I felt entirely happy. Filled to the brim with love, and the knowledge that I had everything I could ever need.

Family. Love. And a bright future with Maddox by my side.

Then there was a knock at the door, and the spell was broken.

"Hello?" I called out, getting to my feet.

The door swung open and one of the pack members, Maverick, stepped into the room. He had a gash above his eye and a bandage wrapped around his shoulder. "Alpha called a meeting. One hour."

His tone was harsh.

I stared after him as he turned and left without another word.

What was that about?

I glanced at my dad who made grumbling noises and shifted on the couch, hoisting himself to the edge. He looked like he was about to stand up.

I put out a hand and pushed against him. "No. You can't get up. You need to give your leg time to heal."

Dad shook his head and pushed himself to his feet. "I'm going to have a quick shower. Then it's time to face the music."

He took a step to test his leg's strength. Then slowly, but with an obvious level of pride in his own resilience, he limped down the hallway.

A shiver of unease wriggled down my spine and I hurried after him.

"What do you mean, face the music?" I grabbed his arm and gently spun him around. "What did you do?"

My dad's mouth twisted. "I told you. I tried to take out their Alpha, and it didn't work."

Tears burned in my eyes, hearing the finality in my dad words. "So? You made a mistake. It's not like there haven't been raids on other packs before; raids that weren't always successful."

"Ah. But this time I made a mistake that cost a lot of other pack members their lives," he said slowly, removing my fingers from his arm.

"But... everyone makes mistakes, Dad. I'm sure they'll forgive you... They always do."

He smiled but didn't say anything else in reply. Instead, he stepped into our small bathroom and shut the door in my face.

I stood in the hallway, my heart filled with worry and my gut tight with dread. What were they going to do to him? Punish him in some way? Toss him out of the pack? Surely they wouldn't do such a thing to *my* father.

He was going to be the next Alpha's father-in-law.

Of course. Excitement grew inside of me at the thought and I rapped on the bathroom door. "I'm going to get changed and find Maddox. I'm sure he'll help. See you at the meeting."

"Okay, sweetie. I love you."

"Love you too!" I yelled, then bolted into my room for a quick change of clothes. Earlier, I'd just thrown a cotton dress over what I'd slept in last night, but I needed to try a bit harder if I was going to convince Maddox to help me.

I had some nearby baby wipes that I used for emergencies, or when the water wasn't running. I did a quick wash of my body, having not showered since last night, and pulled on my black jeans—Maddox's favorite on me—and a tight pink sweater. I took a moment to brush my long hair, because my soon-to-be-husband liked it out and flowing down my back.

Soft and feminine, he said.

I grabbed my house keys and my cell phone, though the coverage out here was terrible, and ran out the door. I had to find Maddox and ask him for support. I had a horrible feeling about what might be about to happen to my dad and I needed to stop it.

My stomach swirled and my heart hammered in my chest the faster I moved my legs. People were everywhere in the streets, walking toward the center of town where the meeting was being held.

The townspeople often told me that my father was well liked by the Alpha. He'd been excused in the past for mistakes that no one else would have gotten away with. I wasn't sure of the details of those mistakes, but whatever had happened in the past, that didn't seem to be the case this time.

I started running toward the Alpha's house. Surely Maddox would be there? I had to find him and beg his help.

And fast.

Chapter 3

Talia

The Alpha's house was locked, and no one was home. I went to Antony's house, Maddox's beta, but still couldn't find anyone.

So, I ran about like a mad woman, searching every house I had access to.

Were they all already at the meeting?

Fuck!

Then the Alpha's booming voice echoed through town. He was projecting his words through the loudspeaker.

"Damn it." I was late to the meeting now, and I hadn't accomplished what I'd set out to do.

I ran toward the center of town. I hadn't kept an eye on the time, and I was sweating from the stress.

My only hope was that my worries were unfounded. Surely the Alpha would pardon my father? He always did. He was a hard Alpha, but not unkind.

Normally.

I reached the edge of the gathering and stopped, taking deep breaths to try and calm myself down. I placed a hand on my heart, feeling the hammering beneath my palm, and took some time to slow my breath.

It's okay. It's going to be okay.

"The attack this morning was... a disaster," the Alpha was saying.

I peered through the crowd, between the heads of the people in front of me. There was a small stage the council had set up for such meetings. It was only two feet off the ground, but it meant that most of us could see whoever was speaking.

My gaze slid from the Alpha, to Maddox, who stood at his father's right, tall and proud, and gorgeous.

My heart leapt in my chest at the sight of my mate. Electricity sizzled in my veins and happiness bubbled through me. There was the person I was meant to spend the rest of my life with.

My love.

My fated mate.

I frowned as I stared at him. Something was different. He wouldn't meet my gaze, even though in the past he would have found me in a crowd this size within moments.

He swayed from foot to foot, and rubbed his hands together as though he was cold.

I was sweating from all the running around. I should have worn a skirt.

I wiped my brow with my forearm and let myself start to relax. It was going to be okay. This was just procedure.

"We lost many souls today. Andrew Murphy, Blaze McGuphry..." The Alpha went on to list more and more men.

So many? There were tears all around, and a loud sob echoed to my left.

My throat closed up, and I swallowed down hard, forcing the tears back. It was such a loss to our pack. So many men. Fathers. Sons. Husbands.

Had my father's mistake caused that? Horror filled me at the realization this might not be something easily forgiven, like in the past.

"We would never have lost so many if it wasn't for the irresponsible actions of a single pack member, Trevor Linetti." The Alpha held out his arm and gestured toward the edge of the stage.

My father stepped up, his face set as he walked resolutely forward.

I put a hand over my mouth to stifle a gasp. What were they going to do to him?

"This is not the first time that Trevor has done something to endanger the pack. Many have wondered why I've spared his life in the past."

There was a murmur of agreement from the pack.

Oh, my God.

I had to get to my dad.

"Excuse me." I pushed through the people in front of me and began to work my way through the crowd. I had to beg them to spare him. I wasn't sure what I'd say, but I had to convince the Alpha not to hurt him.

I shoved through more people, but I was still twenty feet away. The whole pack had turned out for this.

"His wife Margaret was an exceptional woman, and many of you would know that she brought special gifts to the pack. But she is no longer around, and after Trevor's selfish, despicable actions from this morning, I can no longer shield him from the pack's anger."

There was a loud growl and a surge of energy.

"No!" I yelled, and that was when I finally caught my mate's eye. Our gazes connected and I felt the same pull, the same tug of desire and heat that I always did.

"Maddox!"

He looked down and away, breaking our eye contact and ignoring my plea. *No!*

"Trevor Linetti," the Alpha continued, "you are sentenced to death for your crimes against this pack. And your remaining family will be cast out, forbidden from returning, on pain of death."

Sentenced. To death. Oh, my God.

I desperately looked for Maddox again, but he'd moved out of my sight. I didn't care at this moment. I had to get to my father.

I pushed and shoved and ran, stumbling over a woman.

"I'm sorry. Get out of the way. Please!" I screamed out toward the stage. "Dad!"

He didn't turn. Instead, he dropped to his knees in front of the Alpha.

My dad said something I couldn't hear. The Alpha shifted into his massive wolf form in a ripple of light and magic.

"No! Please... No!" I shrieked, throwing myself at the small stage.

The people around me jumped back as if not wanting to touch me. I ploughed forward, falling to my knees just as there was a collective gasp from the crowd and a muffled scream from a woman behind me. A sickening crunch filled my ears and blood spattered everywhere.

Too late.

I reached out for the edge of the stage, gripping the wood with my claws as my wolf shifter rose inside of me, struggling to get out.

I couldn't see, couldn't hear anything but that crunching sound on repeat. Over and over.

My fingers slid in the blood and the tang of it rose to fill my nostrils.

I tried not to vomit as I stared at the mangled body on the stage.

The Alpha had just killed my father.

Right in front of my eyes.

I RAN THROUGH THE WOODS in my shifter form. How I got here, I had no idea. Trees flew past as images of my father's headless, lifeless body dropping to the stage floor echoed in my mind.

It had to be a dream.

No. A nightmare.

A nightmare to end all nightmares.

I couldn't have designed a worse fate for myself. My only living family... gone. The man I loved—the man I was *mated* to—standing by, watching and doing nothing, as his father killed mine.

Romeo and Juliet had nothing on me.

I ran and ran, until my legs gave out and I collapsed onto the grass. The sunshine danced in my fur, making a mockery of my sorrow.

I was going to be sick. How dare the sun even show its head on a day like today?

It was the end of my life as I knew it.

Dad was gone. *Dead*. And I was to be banished from the pack. My own pack. Casting me out at the moment I was most in need.

And Maddox... My thoughts skittered away. I couldn't bear to think of his betrayal in this moment.

I closed my eyes, waves of grief washing over me. The devastation was so complete, my anger couldn't even try to rear its head.

My father had done what his Alpha had asked of him, and that same Alpha had thought it his duty, his *right*, to end my father's life.

What was I going to do now?

My ears pricked up at the sound of running. Two sets of paws hitting the earth, if my ears were correct.

Were the pack coming for me already? Was I to be put to death as well? The week before my wedding.

I didn't even care right now. They could take me and I would join my parents. At least then I wouldn't be alone.

I didn't even lift my head, just rolled onto my side and stayed there, waiting for fate to deliver the death blow.

The running grew closer, followed by the panting breath of two wolves.

I refused to open my eyes, the pain in my heart making me wish I could crawl into a dark hole and die.

Literally.

There was a ripple of magic, and a shift in the air. Then two sets of human hands were on me.

"Talia! Are you okay?" Nyssa asked, pressing a kiss onto the top of my head.

"Of course, she's not okay, you idiot!" Celia practically yelled at her. "Did you see what the Alpha did! Did you hear what he said?"

I hadn't realized how much I wanted to cry, until this moment. As my sadness became overwhelming, my wolf shifter let go, and my human body returned.

The forest was cold, and my friends' hands were warm on my skin.

"Oh, my God." I began to sob, letting the tears finally fall.

I curled up into a ball and rocked as I vocalized all my pain, while my two friends wrapped their arms around me. I screamed and cried, and howled, and still they held me.

Eventually, the tears dried up, and I was left feeling like a husk of a person, unwilling and unable to form a single coherent thought. Or feel anything other than darkness.

"The pack's isolation cabin is not far from here. Let's go there and get warm," Nyssa said softly.

I shook my head, not able to answer.

"Come on, Talia. Up you get," Celia coaxed, putting one arm around my back and somehow managing to get me onto my feet.

My knees gave way.

"Grab the other side," Celia called, and Nyssa pressed in close.

If it had been any other time, I would have remarked on the strangeness of their naked bodies pressed against mine. But this was not the time for lighthearted jests.

Instead, their closeness kept my heart from breaking completely.

They half-carried me through the woods, my feet dragging in the dirt and forest floor debris.

"Put me down. Please. I just can't..."

My voice was hoarse and my stomach was empty. Had I vomited at some stage? I didn't remember. Everything back at the pack grounds was dark after that moment...

"No," Celia hissed. "We are not staying out here, naked and alone. We are getting to the cabin so we can get some clothes and talk about what we're going to do next."

The vehemence behind her words bolstered my strength and I somehow managed to get my feet under me and join them in the awkward stagger to our new destination.

Finally.... finally, I saw the wooden cabin through the trees.

"We're almost there, Talia," Nyssa said, breathing hard. "Almost there."

Together, all three of us, like some naked, four-legged race, clung to each other as we aimed for the cabin.

When we finally staggered up the front steps and stood on the stoop, Nyssa pushed open the door and we fell in.

Celia groaned as she staggered to a nearby couch and I hit the deck, crawling over to the bear skin rug in front of the cold fireplace.

"Give me a minute. I'll light a fire," Nyssa said, her teeth chattering.

I lifted my head and stared out the window. The sun was beginning to fall out of the sky, and shadows crossed the window.

Just how long had I been out in the forest alone?

Celia grunted as she heaved herself up off the couch. "I'm gonna lock the door, then find us some clothes."

She slid the large bolt into the deadlock, then started going through the cupboards lining the walls.

"Got it!" Nyssa said, and I managed to pull myself up into a sitting position as the first flickers of flame in the cold grate began to burn.

I swallowed against the dryness in my throat. "I haven't been here in... forever." I couldn't even remember the last time I had run as far as this. Several years, at least.

The cabin was a large box with no internal walls. There were beds against one wall, kitchen stuff on the opposite side, and all the living area in the middle where we currently sat.

There was a toilet outside, but I wasn't venturing out there right this minute.

"Yeah, I haven't been here in a while, either," Nyssa said, settling cross-legged beside me and staring into the flames.

The fire was growing by the minute and my once goose-bumped skin was beginning to warm.

"Here," Celia said, throwing some clothes in our direction. "There's sweaters and jeans, and a few tops. Not exactly our sizes, but at least we'll be warm."

The clothes she'd thrown at me were for a man, four times as big as I needed. But I slipped on the huge sweater with relief, and tucked my bare legs up inside and lay my head on my knees.

There was a long silence before Nyssa finally put her hand on my back. "What are you going to do, Talia?"

I sighed, all my tears dried up. "I don't know. I really don't know."

"You're the next Alpha's fated mate. Surely they'll take you back," Celia said, coming to sit down next to me on the bear skin rug and stretching out in front of the fire.

I squeezed my knees even harder. "I hope so. We're fated mates... right? No one rejects their mate."

My question was answered by silence, so I finally lifted my head and repeated my question. "Right?"

Chapter 4

Talia

I stared at Celia, the stronger of my two friends. The harsher one. The physically bigger one. She'd never shied away from telling it to me straight.

"Celia?"

She pressed her lips into a firm line, then nodded. "You're right. No one has ever walked away from their mate. You guys are fated! Nothing would mess that up."

Nyssa shuffled forward so we were sitting in a sort of triangle, and I could see both of them. "How are you feeling about it all though? Like, Maddox's dad killed your dad. How are you going to... get past that?"

I didn't have an answer to that one.

"I just want Maddox," I said. "I want him to come here, and wrap me up in his arms, and tell me everything's going to be okay."

Celia and Nyssa glanced at each other, then converged on me like they had out in the forest, holding me close.

I didn't fight them. I allowed them to press even harder into me, closed my eyes, and inhaled their mingled earthy scent.

"We'll never leave you," Nyssa said. "You're our best friend, no matter what."

"Always," Celia added. "You can count on us."

We climbed into the bed without dinner and somehow, exhaustion took me. We slept through the night.

When I woke up in the morning, the birds were singing in the trees surrounding the cabin, and faint rays of sunlight filtered into the room.

I pushed the scratchy blanket off me and stretched, my stomach rumbling for food.

"Morning," Celia said, though she was a grouch in the morning.

"How are you feeling?" Nyssa asked, sitting up and staring at me like I would do something stupid if she dared take her eyes off me for a single minute.

"Um... hungry," I said. "And... ready to go back."

I still felt strangely numb in my mind. Like someone had slammed down a huge wall between my memories and me. I couldn't feel much except for an aching in my chest, like I had a hole in my ribcage.

I lifted my hand and rubbed at the spot over my heart where my father's love used to sit. "I need to go back and see what they've done with my dad, and I really need to see Maddox and find out what we're going to do."

"Let's get going ASAP, then," Celia said.

Nyssa nodded. "We need food too."

We all took off the clothes we'd borrowed, folded them up, and shut the door to keep the wild animals out of the cabin.

"Let's do it," Celia said.

It was time to go home, so we shifted back into our wolf forms for traveling.

Nyssa and Celia were both a nice gray, but I'd always been black. Just like my mother.

Together, as a small pack of three wolves, we ran home. When we hit the main road in our town, we all went our separate ways to find our houses and get clothes.

When I reached my home, I shifted as soon as I stepped onto the porch.

My heart was in my throat as I opened the door, the words stuck in my head as I fought the desire to call out to my dad. To ask how his night was and tell him about mine.

I glanced around the room. It was like nothing had changed. Like he wasn't dead.

I rushed to my bedroom, running from the memory of what had happened yesterday, a whirlwind of emotions set to chase after me if I dared to think on it too long. They would drag me into the pit of despair if I gave them half a chance.

I had the fastest shower on record, but one was needed, nonetheless. I was covered in sweat and tears and dirt; I was pretty sure neither Maddox nor the Alpha would be happy about that if I were to turn up on their doorstep, unwashed.

Then I dressed, not sure if I needed to be getting ready for a funeral, or not. So, I reached for my most comfortable pair of black leggings, a long dress, and a heavy silver belt.

I walked out of the house without a backward glance, tears in my eyes and emotion clogging my throat. Yesterday had been the worst day of my life, bar none. Surely, today couldn't be any worse?

People stared at me as I walked down the main street in our small village.

We were about a fifteen-minute drive away from the main town we all frequented. Our closed shifter community made it safe for us to live the way we needed to, but also kept us close enough to civilization for access to school and shops.

The closer I walked to the Alpha's house, the more people stared at me. Members of a community I'd known my whole life were pointing at me. A few people shot glares my way.

What had I done wrong? I was the one whose only family had been brutally killed by our Alpha.

That thought made me resolutely stomp forward.

The Alpha's house was the biggest in town. Double-story, with huge windows, a large wooden door, and an imposing brick façade.

I lifted my chin and marched up the steps. I didn't know what I was going to say, but I could already sense that begging was on the cards.

The biggest question in my mind though was, what was Maddox going to do? Surely he'd be on my side in this. He didn't like to go up against his father. But that was because he was a good son, and a loyal pack member. Not because he didn't love me.

I lifted my hand to knock on the door. It flew open before I had the chance to touch it. I stared at the man standing in the doorway.

"Hello, Talia."

I swallowed hard. "Maddox. I've come to talk to your dad. Is he home?"

My mate nodded. "Yeah. He is. Come in. I wasn't sure if you'd left already."

"Left?" I repeated as I walked inside.

Maddox shut the door behind me.

He didn't answer, but simply ushered me into the large living room where his father sat on the couch. Three of his council members stood behind him.

My stomach dropped, and I reached for Maddox for comfort.

He shook my grasping hand off his arm and marched away.

I couldn't help the soft cry that ripped from my throat. "Maddox... don't walk away. Please... I..."

Maddox kept walking, until he was around the couch and standing at his father's right side.

When he turned to stare at me, his face was stone cold.

I gasped and pressed my hand to my mouth. I was supposed to get married this week. To the man standing right in front of me, staring at me as if I was a stranger. I was going to spend my life devoted to him, loving him, raising his children.

I didn't understand why he was acting like this.

"I don't..." I shook my head, and then dragged my gaze down to his father when he made an annoyed noise in his throat.

The Alpha might have been the only one seated on the couch, but his presence dominated the room. "Talia Linetti, I told you yesterday. You are no longer a member of this pack. You are banished. I will allow you seventy-two hours to leave town and get across state lines, or the pack will hunt you down and deliver to you the same fate that befell your father."

My mouth gaped open, unwanted tears filling my eyes and spilling down my cheeks despite my best efforts to hold them in. "But... I'm supposed to get married next week. To... Maddox. How... why...?"

The words tumbled from my lips, yet I had no real idea what I was saying. My world had tipped on its axis and I had nothing concrete to hold onto.

The Alpha stood and I craned my neck to look up at his six-foot-six frame, fear shivering through me. Even at his advanced age, he was the most dangerous man I'd ever seen.

"I will leave you and my son to speak, but my word is law. You will never return here, Talia. Your father was a disgrace, and you will take his shame to your grave."

The Alpha turned to leave.

I forced my voice to work, though it sounded rusty and weak. "Where is my father, Alpha? His body? I would like to see him one more time. Say... goodbye."

My lip trembled as I spoke, and I bit it hard. I felt like a pathetic child acting so terrified in this moment. But he was the most powerful man in my pack, and he had just murdered my father.

"He's been taken to the pack's burial site," the Alpha said, and walked out without another look.

His betas, the other three men in the room, all left with him.

As soon as the door shut, I staggered toward my mate. I landed on my knees on the couch, staring directly at Maddox standing behind the furniture.

A pained sob wrenched itself from my chest as I stared at my husband-to-be. "Tell me I'm dreaming. That I'm in a nightmare and one day I'm going to wake up from this. Maddox. Please…"

I reached out for him once more, for his gorgeous, perfect hands, desperate for comfort from my mate, but he pulled away, out of my reach.

No! Please.

"Talia. Stop. You heard the Alpha." Maddox turned his back on me, his ass making his jeans looked way sexier than he had any right to at this point in time.

"But we're fated!" I pushed myself to my feet. "You and I are meant to be! You've said it a thousand times. It's why we're getting married. It's why we waited so long…"

I gulped down the words, bitterness lacing my tongue.

What *was* the reason we'd waited so long? If we were mates…

Some mates couldn't wait even a minute to start fucking. They saw each other, and that was it. *Boom.* They were together from that moment on. But Maddox and I had dated for years. He said he'd wanted to wait until our wedding night to finally take me.

I'd always thought it was the most romantic thing I'd ever known. A shifter who would fight his most basic instincts to show respect for his partner. To wait until our official mating to impregnate me.

But maybe it had been more than that?

Maddox shook his head. "It doesn't matter."

"Of course, it matters!"

He stared at the wall opposite him, as if he couldn't bear to look at me anymore.

I stumbled around the couch and stood in front of him, forcing his gaze onto me. "Maddox! I love you. We have to find a way to change your father's mind."

His jaw tightened and his teeth set in that obstinate way he'd had since we were young.

"No, Talia." His eyes were cold. Empty. "I reject our bond, and I reject you. We will never be mated."

Chapter 5

Talia

I stared up at Maddox, dumbstruck. "No. You can't. A wolf only has one mate. You'll never have another... I'll never have another. It's not how it works."

He started to crack, a small hint of the man I had known beginning to shine through in his sad smile and the pain in his beautiful blue eyes.

Finally, he took my hands in his and gripped them tight. "We don't have a choice, Talia. The Alpha's word is law. You know that."

"But..."

"No buts," Maddox said, then pulled me into a tight hug.

I breathed in his scent, inhaling deeply. And it was all there. The familiar woodsy smell. The sweetness of his cologne.

I began to cry. "This is so unfair."

And it was. All of it.

I couldn't possibly lose my father and my mate in the same twenty-four-hour period. Could I? Fate would never be that cruel.

He pulled back from the hug and shoved me away.

I stumbled then pushed forward, seeking the reassurance of the man who'd been my boyfriend, my mate, for three years now. "Please, Maddox... please..."

He strode to the door and opened it.

When he glanced back, there was pain and regret written all over his face. "I'm so sorry about your dad. I tried to help, but..."

He shrugged.

I nodded. I knew. He was helpless to change his father's mind while his dad was still the Alpha.

"Go and see your dad," Maddox said quietly, "Goodbye Talia."

I raised a hand to beckon him. "Madd—"

The door closed and I was alone in the room.

Rejected.

It was unheard of. Impossible. I shook my head, and a wave of unexpected pain coursed through me. My head felt like it was about to explode from the stress and grief. I staggered a little from the impact of the sudden headache, clinging to the couch so that I didn't pass out. That was the last thing I needed, to give the Alpha another reason to hate me.

Adrenaline rippled down my legs and I found myself propelled forward by a will that didn't even feel like my own.

I needed to see my dad. And then I had to get the hell out of here.

My trembling legs moved me forward, through the town and toward the cemetery. Where would they have put him?

I glanced around, terrified of what I was about to see. How would my father's body look after a night out in the elements?

Then I saw it. The newly dug grave, in a familiar spot. I stumbled over to the headstone I had knelt at for over ten years, my mother's final resting place.

There, now beside her, was a new burial. The dirt was freshly turned over and instead of a tombstone, there was simple wooden cross planted in the ground.

No words. No name.

He had been buried as a traitor.

An angry sob rose in my throat, so I tried to concentrate on the one thing they had managed to get right. He'd been buried beside my mom. His mate. The love of his life.

The tears flowed freely again, down my face in hot, wet torrents. I wiped them away with the back of my hand, numb to most of the feelings now. But my tears wouldn't stop.

They didn't even let me say a proper goodbye to him.

I stayed there, on my knees, in the dirt, until my legs ached from the position and my face was finally dry.

When I could stand, I pushed myself up and began the slow, painful walk of shame back home. Through the streets of our town, past the homes and judgmental glances of the pack that now shunned me. Away from the mate that rejected me. I walked until I fell in my father's front door and then I simply lay on the floorboards until morning.

GALEN

I stepped into my father's bedroom and hurried to his bedside.

"Son. You have news?" he asked, pushing himself up and leaning back against the pillows.

"You don't look well, Father." I couldn't help the words. His cheeks were ashen and sunken. His eyes, dark holes in his head.

He was no longer the strong Alpha I had grown up with, and I had no idea how to stop the decline.

"Don't worry about me, Galen," he said, swatting his hand through the air in a dismissive gesture. "I'm stronger than I look. Always have been. Now, tell me what happened this morning."

He didn't reprimand me for not waking him, and for that I was grateful. I didn't want to admit to the truth—that I hadn't dared wake him because he was so unwell and weak that I didn't want him in the fight.

"The Northwood pack attacked at sunrise."

My father's dark brows lowered. "Bastards. What happened?"

I inhaled sharply. I'd spent hours with my men after the fight, assessing their injuries, sitting with them as they were stitched and bandaged. Pouring alcohol over wounds, and down throats for pain management.

Wolf shifters were strong, deadly creatures, but we were still mortal.

"Three dead, ten badly wounded. But we won the fight."

My dad's eyes glittered with anger. "You need to make them pay, Galen. This cannot stand."

I nodded. I knew that revenge would be on the cards, but how strong a force my father wanted, I didn't know.

"We killed at least ten of their men. Their pack won't be nearly as strong as it once was."

My father sat up in his bed. "Serves them bloody right! Coming here to fight us on our own lands, totally unprovoked." He shook his head and tsked loudly. "Their Alpha must have rocks in his head."

"The men want to retaliate," I said, about to speak further until I saw my father's tiredness sweep over him. I stopped talking.

He leaned back once again, exhausted from this mysterious sickness that no one could name.

"You should do that, Galen. You are our Alpha in my stead."

I stood up, staring down at the strongest man I'd ever known. "I'll speak to them, Father. We need to formulate a plan. I'll see you later."

I headed for the door.

My father chuckled. "You don't have to sleep here at the house, son. I might be unwell but I don't need a babysitter."

I grunted. "The bar doesn't need a babysitter, either. My apartment can wait."

My father closed his eyes and I slid out, shutting the door quietly behind me.

Until my father relinquished his role, or passed on from this life, he was our Alpha. He lived in the Alpha's house, where I had grown up.

I owned a bar in town, about twenty minutes away, and I lived in the apartment above. It was a hectic life, but I loved it, and running the bar passed the time between pack obligations.

I walked down the hall and out the front door, where I was met by three of my Beta wolves.

David, Markus, and Theo.

"Hey, guys."

"We need to plan how we're going to get them back," Theo said, puffing up his chest.

I waved my hand. "Follow me. We'll go to the meeting hall and talk there."

The guys fell into line behind me, and we walked down the main street of our pack's town until we reached the small hall where we held weddings, funerals, and birthdays.

I opened the front door and entered the currently empty space. "Pull up a chair and let's get this party going."

I grabbed one of the chairs stacked against the wall, dragged it into the center of the room, and sat down.

The other three guys did the same. The Betas were my oldest friends. We'd gone to school together, hunted together, chased girls together, and now we sat and planned a war together.

It was strange the way some things changed, and others stayed the same.

When everyone was settled, I took the opportunity to study them. Most of them were uninjured from this morning's fight, except for Markus, whose eyebrow was covered in dried blood, and his neck had a neat row of stitches showing above his collar bone.

I swallowed hard, an ache forming in my gut. These men would put their lives on the line in a heartbeat, to keep our pack safe.

I was grateful more of the pack weren't injured, but I dreaded the fights to come.

"So," I said, "tell me what you're thinking."

The guys glanced at each other, then Theo moved forward, pinning me with an intense stare. "We need to pay them back. Like... now."

I held a hand up to calm him. "We do, and we will. Going right now, without a solid plan, would not be smart. We killed a lot of their pack..."

"Which leaves them vulnerable!" David hissed. "We should strike now."

I shook my head, my gaze sliding over to Markus, and the way he shifted uncomfortably in his seat. Did he agree with the others?

I focused back on David. "Our pack has been hurt too. We don't want to go off half-cocked and get more of our friends killed because we didn't wait for them to heal."

David lifted his chin in a show of defiance. "Wolves heal fast."

I sighed. "I know. So, you don't need to be patient long. A few days, a week maybe, and we'll be back to full force."

"Except for Damian, and Toby," Markus said quietly.

"And Rocko," Theo added.

Our fallen comrades. We'd been lucky to only lose three men, but it was still three too many, for a fight we had neither expected, nor started.

Anger pooled in my gut. We would get our vengeance, for our men.

I leaned back in my chair. "God rest their souls. Have their burials been arranged?"

Markus nodded. "The pack has decided to do one funeral a day for the next three days, so their families have time to prepare, and mourn."

That was a good idea, rather than forcing the pack to attend all three funerals in one day.

I clapped my hands together. "So, we allow ourselves a week to heal, and prepare for war."

The three Betas nodded, in agreement with my timeline at last. "We should increase our security," Theo said, "in case they try something again."

I shot him an approving look. "You're right. We'll double it. Four men on watch every shift from tonight."

That would stretch our numbers a little, but it would just mean covering people in their day jobs when those on watch duty needed to sleep.

"So, when do we attack?" David asked, the bloodthirsty question making me want to roll my eyes.

That sort of dumb thinking had gotten the other pack's members killed.

"We don't, necessarily. We need to be smarter than them."

"What do you mean?" Theo asked.

"I think we need to do more than just walk onto their land and start another fight," I began. "I don't know what, exactly. But there has to be a better way to seek vengeance than just copying their own stupid move. If we just do the same as they did, the outcome will be similar, until finally there'll be no men left in either pack."

"Then what do you suggest?" Markus asked.

I spread my hands wide. "I don't know yet, but there's gotta be a better way. Throw any ideas at me that you have."

There was a long moment of silence and I could almost hear the cogs in their brains turning.

"What about kidnapping the son of the Alpha?" Theo said. "He's a wanker. I've seen him in town. Big guy, but weak. He's a coward."

"Really? Tell me more…"

We spent the rest of the afternoon throwing ideas around.

By the time the sun was setting over the forest, we were finally done and had a few ideas on how we might be able to cripple the pack nearest us.

I'd always hoped the war we fought on this soil for generations would end with me, but here I was, not even in the shoes of the Alpha yet, and I was planning my first attack.

I didn't like the idea of it. But this pack meant everything to me. And I would defend all of our pack members with my life, even if it meant going on the offensive.

I lumbered back to the Alpha's house, unwilling to leave my dad and go home to my apartment just yet. He seemed weaker every time I saw him, which was so frustrating. It was unusual—almost unheard of—for a wolf to die of sickness.

Especially an Alpha.

We died of heartbreak, or injuries sustained while fighting, or an accident like my mother. Simple old age was the most common, when our hearts gave out, but wolf shifters lived far longer than humans. We did not die of some strange unidentifiable disease in our fifties.

My father hadn't seen me mated, hadn't met his grandchildren. It was unfathomable to me that, at thirty years old, I may lose my remaining parent.

Our Alpha. Supposed to be the strongest of us all.

I crept into the house and checked out the fridge. It was stocked full of ready-made meals and I smiled. Our pack looked after one another. The wives of Father's council would have made these meals.

Lasagna, stew, pasta, and rice dishes.

They'd been cooking for him since my mother had passed, and I had to assume the care had only increased since he'd been ill.

"Galen? That you?"

I turned toward my father's voice. "Yeah, Dad. Thought I'd stay here tonight."

"You raiding the fridge?" he called out.

I laughed. There was nothing wrong with his hearing.

"Yeah. There's some lasagna here that looks good. You want some?"

"Sure. Bring me a plate."

I smiled as I heated the food in the microwave. A healthy appetite was a good sign he was feeling better.

On the days when he didn't eat, it wasn't good. I could see the pain in his face on those days. They were the worst.

I took the food and went to sit with Dad in his room.

I inhaled my dinner, not even realizing how hungry I was until I glanced up and found he'd barely taken more than a few bites.

"Good?" Dad asked, a smile in his tone despite the still-full plate.

I grinned, trying to keep things as normal as possible. "Yeah. Very good." The cheese sauce was creamy, the meat rich, and the pasta cooked to perfection. "Nancy's recipe?"

My dad chuckled. "Yeah. Good guess."

Nancy lived next door and was married to my dad's oldest friend.

I set down my plate and he handed me his. "Finish mine off too. I don't need to eat anymore. I'm full."

My stomach dropped and I set his plate aside. I couldn't do that. Not now. "Dad..."

"I need you to promise me something, Galen."

I leaned forward. "Anything."

Whatever my dad wanted, I would do.

"You have to promise me that you'll avenge the pack. This morning's attack was a sign that news of my sickness has gotten out. The other packs think we're weak. Vulnerable. You can't let them get away with it. It will..." My father stopped to cough. "It will..." He coughed again.

"It's okay, Dad."

He shook his head. "It's not okay, Galen. When an Alpha dies, and his son resumes the new role, it's the most common time to attack another pack. It is considered the easiest time to take over. But you have to show them all that we are still strong. I know you can do this. You *are* strong. A born leader."

My breath caught in my throat, and I forced a laugh. "You're not dying yet, old man."

He smiled at me, and behind his eyes, there was an ocean of pain. "Not today. But it won't be long, Galen. You have to promise me that you won't let them take over our pack, *your* pack. Your legacy. You need to strike back while you can."

"Dad, I..."

"Promise me." My father growled.

The hairs on the back on my neck stood on end as I offered up the only words my father wanted to hear.

"I promise, Dad. I'll avenge our fallen men. They won't take this pack from me. No one will."

Then I closed my eyes and hung my head, the weight of the world on my shoulders.

Chapter 6

Talia

I had three days to leave town, forever. Three days to leave behind everything I had ever known and loved.

Today was officially the worst day of my life. And I had horrendously bad days to compare it to.

The day my mother had died.

The day my father had been killed.

And now, the day I'd been ousted from the pack I'd grown up with *and* the day I'd been rejected by my fated mate.

I slept on the floor of the lounge room at my dad's house the night before, unable to get up. I could barely move. I hadn't eaten in so long my stomach felt like it was consuming itself.

I still didn't want to eat. I wanted to cry. And curl into a ball and stay there.

So, I did.

I went to bed, pulled the covers over my head, and woke up to the sound of a rooster crowing, and a loud knock at the front door.

I sat up, bleary eyed and confused.

What day was it? What was I meant to be doing... *Oh*.

Reality hit me with the force of a two-by-four piece of wood. Thump. Right across the chest, making my ribs squeeze tight and my heart drop to the base of my stomach with a sickening lurch.

I now had two days to get out, to leave my pack... forever. It was an unfathomable reality. I put my hand to my head. The headache had come back in force.

The knock on the door came again.

"Talia! Open up."

I scrambled out of bed to the sound of Celia's no-nonsense voice. I raced to the front door, tripping over my own feet, and wrenched the door open.

"Celia."

She looked me up and down, then charged inside past me. "We need to find you somewhere to stay, some clean clothes, and some money. Have you got access to anything of your dad's?"

Nyssa was standing behind Celia, her eyes full of tears. "I'm so sorry, Talia."

Then she put her arms around me and hugged me tight.

I couldn't stop my own tears as they welled up and coursed down my cheeks. Damn it. I'd thought I'd run out of those.

I pulled out of my friend's comforting arms and reached for the front door, shutting it behind Nyssa and then locking it for good measure.

"What were you saying, Celia?" I asked, wiping the tears from my face. I loved Nyssa, and a large part of me wanted to wallow in her care and affection, but I was more in need of Celia's no-nonsense guidance and help.

She was level-headed and I needed that right now.

"You need a shower, and you need to pack. Essentials, mostly. Your favorite clothes. Photos. Jewelry. Things that you can't replace."

I nodded. She was right. I had my dad's old car to travel in, so I could fill that up with stuff. But there wasn't a lot of room in the little hatchback. Especially since I had no idea where I was supposed to go.

"Okay." I blinked. My brain was foggy. "So, my first step is to pack?"

Celia and Nyssa exchanged a worried look.

Then Celia took a deep breath. "No. You shower. Nyssa, make Talia something to eat while she's showering, and pack whatever food is portable. We need a plan. I'll start packing clothes. I pretty much know everything you own."

I couldn't help smiling a little. She probably did. We spent so much time together, Celia would have seen everything I'd ever owned.

"Thanks, guys."

Celia flapped her hands at me. "Go. Shower. And wash your hair. You're a mess. I'll meet you in your bedroom after you're done."

A sense of calm settled over me. I could deal with my pain and my grief, later. For now, I was following Lieutenant Celia's instructions. "Yes, ma'am."

I went straight to the bathroom, stripped off the clothes I'd slept in, and climbed into the hot shower. Celia was right. I was a mess. Covered in dirt, grime, snot and tears, and with my brain only on half-power. Hopefully the hot water would help kick start the latter, at least.

Turns out I was numb to the normal pleasure of a hot shower. Instead, I mechanically moved, doing what Celia wanted, but no more.

I scrubbed myself clean, washed my hair, and climbed out. I managed to wrap a towel around my head and body, before Celia stuck her head in the door.

"I'm packing your clothes. You grab some toiletries. Toothpaste and toothbrush. Toilet paper too."

Then she was gone again.

"Toilet paper?" I repeated, then shrugged and grabbed a few rolls and packed my small toiletry bag.

I'd bought all new stuff for my honeymoon next week, suitcases and everything, but they were locked away in my father's bedroom, and I wasn't going anywhere near that space.

I wasn't sure I could handle the reminder of where my life should have been headed, but instead had taken an abrupt turn toward Hell.

"Keep it together," I whispered to myself as I picked up what I needed from the bathroom and headed to my bedroom.

Celia had turned the place upside down. There were clothes everywhere as she went through every item, packing what she thought I might need neatly into a black suitcase on the floor.

"Have you got more bags? Another suitcase maybe?" she asked.

"Um. I have a backpack or two, I think."

"Get them."

I grabbed what she wanted from the cupboard, then moved over to my clothes and stared at the pile.

What to wear on the day I escaped my pack?

"Wear something comfortable to drive in, and warm," Celia said. "You have to be over state lines by tomorrow night, so you'll be driving most of the day, I'd say."

I nodded, turning away to hide the tears that welled in my eyes.

I grabbed for an old comfortable pair of blue denim jeans, a black tank, and a gray sweater.

"Boots?" I asked her.

Celia wrinkled her nose. "I'll pack those. You wear sneakers."

She went back to dissecting my wardrobe.

I dressed and tried not to think.

"Talia!" Nyssa called from the kitchen. "Come eat!"

I glanced at Celia who waved me away. "Go. Go. We're on a time clock, here."

I groaned and trudged to the kitchen.

My heart was beginning to pump a little harder, a little faster now. It hadn't given up on me, which was a good thing.

I think.

"There wasn't a lot in here," Nyssa said, placing a plate down in front of me loaded with toast, scrambled eggs, bacon, and tomatoes. Despite her protest, the plate looked more than enough, to me. I was still struggling to get my stomach working again. It was full of anxiety and grief and there wasn't much room for food.

"I did the best I could," she added, and I sent her a grateful smile.

"Thank you, Nyssa."

She nodded at me, her eyes filling with tears, before she turned away to the pantry. "I found a box in the recycling and I'm going to fill it with food you can eat while driving, and some canned goods and stuff. And I'll make you some sandwiches as well, 'cause I know you forget to feed yourself, if there's no one else to cook for."

I shrugged. "It's better when there are others to feed. Makes it worthwhile."

She glanced over her shoulder and grinned at me. "I agree! So, eat!"

I picked up my fork and knife and slowly began to consume what she'd put on my plate. On a normal day, I would have devoured the whole lot, but my stomach ached after the first few bites. I forced myself to keep going. I hadn't eaten at all yesterday, and I needed my strength if I was getting out of here alive.

I shoved more food down my throat, until I was almost gagging on the bacon.

"Thank you," I said, pushing the half empty plate toward Nyssa.

She popped her head up from where she was kneeling on the floor, going through the cupboards. "That's more than I expected. I'm going to pack you a little bit of cutlery, and plates, and glasses, and stuff." She glanced at her watch. "We've only got half an hour or so left before you should be on the road. Is there anything personal you want to take with you?"

I opened my mouth to ask her why they both seemed to think I had to get out of the house this morning. Didn't I have another forty-eight hours?

"Um, yeah."

"Then go grab it," Nyssa said with a weak smile.

I took a steadying breath and headed to my father's bedroom, where my mother's jewelry was stored along with the photo albums my father had kept close to him.

I ran my hand over my parents' wedding bed. I'd always thought I'd live in this town, with my pack, until the day I died. I couldn't believe I was being forced out, through no fault of my own. And that my father was no longer with me in this life.

A pang shot through my heart and I bowed my head to hide the rush of emotion.

"Do you need a bag to put those things in?" Nyssa called.

I snapped out of my fog and turned toward the door. "No, I'll take Dad's suitcase with me. It's all good."

It wasn't, but I was trying to keep my head above water, lest the depression drown me.

I grabbed my dad's travel bag and packed everything I could see that was literally irreplaceable. Photos. Jewelry. Then I remembered where all the certificates were. The deed to the house. My birth certificate. Surely that stuff was important, too?

I ran down the hallway and into the small study that was once my nursery. There, in a small set of drawers, was everything my father deemed important.

I grabbed the various papers and stored them in my dad's black bag. Maybe one day I'd be able to come back here.

When I walked back into the kitchen, the front door was open and Celia was taking boxes of clothes to the car, packing them in the back seat and the trunk.

"Grab your quilt, too," she called from the car. "You know, the one your mom made."

"Oh, yeah." I couldn't believe I'd forgotten it.

I ran back to my room and opened my blanket box, pulling out the hand sewn quilt my mom had made for me for my eighth birthday. Not long before she died.

I wrapped it up and headed outside. Nyssa packed a box of food and several plastic bags into my car.

"You guys are really wanting me to leave, huh?" I asked, trying to make it sound like a joke.

But then Nyssa released a sob, and guilt washed over me.

I rushed toward her. "I didn't mean it like that!"

She wrapped her arms around me and I squeezed her tight, feeling like, for the first time, I was having to comfort her instead of the other way around.

"I'm going to miss you so much," she said.

"Aren't you guys going to come with me to town, at least?" I asked. "We could have a farewell lunch... or..."

Nyssa pulled out of my arms and took a step back toward Celia. They looked at each other, and Nyssa said, "We can't."

Celia handed me the car keys, then took out her wallet. "I've scrounged up everything I could find for you."

She pulled out a wad of cash.

I put my hands up and refused to take it. "I don't need that. I can get a job. Work my way across the state."

She moved closer, folded the cash over and pushed it into my jeans pocket. "You're gonna need gas, and food, and a place to stay. The money was meant to be a wedding present so... yeah."

Celia stepped back, thrust her hands into her jean pockets, and pressed her lips into a thin line.

Tears welled in her eyes, and I bit down on the inside of my cheek to stop from crying. "Why can't you come with me?"

I wasn't sure I wanted the answer, but I also needed to know for sure.

"The Alpha," Nyssa said quietly. "We've been banned from helping you, and we're under orders to hunt you down if you're not gone by sunrise on Thursday."

I shivered at the threat behind the words. The Alpha's, not Nyssa's.

"But you already did help me." I gestured to the house. "You packed me up and..."

I trailed off. They were helping to get rid of me.

"Oh. You were just making sure I away on time."

Nyssa shook her head. "It's not like that. We convinced the Alpha to let us help you pack up. We told him we could make you leave faster, but that's not why we did it. We don't want you hurt, Talia. You're our best friend. We wanted to help you, and... send you on your way with the knowledge that we love and care for you."

Nyssa's voice broke on the last word, and Celia wrapped an arm around her. I nodded once, appreciating their motives. But it was time to go.

"Okay. I'll call you when I arrive... wherever I'm going."

Celia opened the car door for me.

"There's more money in the glove compartment," she whispered.

I actually managed to laugh, the sound rusty and painful in my throat as I slid into the driver's seat. Laughing was far better than crying, and I had already done so much of that in the past couple of days. "I'll see you guys later, I guess."

The girls smiled as they shut the car door. I started the engine.

I had no idea where I was going, but I put the car into gear and drove away. Away from the only family, and the only home, I'd ever known.

Chapter 7

Talia

I only had one human friend in town, Kylie. We worked together at the restaurant I waitressed at for extra money on the weekends.

Part of me considered just filling up the tank with gas and driving until I ran out of fuel. I could head for the state line right now and not look back. After all, I had cash, and food, and a blanket if I decided to sleep in the car.

But every instinct told me to take a little more time and not just run off with no plan in my head. I needed to work out a plan of action. I decided to stop in town and speak to Kylie, and get organized. I needed to pull money out of the bank and do a little shopping for supplies. I had two days after all, before the Alpha's deadline.

And what was my rush to get somewhere else? It wasn't like I had anywhere else to go. I was completely alone and helpless in this shit storm.

I drove the fifteen minutes to town, gripping the steering wheel of my dad's old car and glancing down at the yellow light on the gas gauge every minute or so.

I'd definitely need gas before I went anywhere else, that was certain.

When I hit the edge of town, I slowed as I drove down the main road. I had to find Kylie, and the best place to start was the restaurant we worked at. I'd go from there.

She'd given me her cell number ages ago, but my phone was AWOL as of yesterday, and I had no idea where it was, or if I'd ever get it back.

Better to start fresh. I'd buy a new one, get a new number, then contact Celia and Nyssa when I'd crossed the state line and was safe.

I shook my head.

Safe from the clutches of my own pack, who'd been told to hunt me down and kill me if I didn't get away. How ludicrous. How terrifying. That people who I had considered family, would kill me just because of a mistake my father had made...

I shook my head, trying not to follow that thought any further, and pulled into an empty spot outside the restaurant. There were a few people inside, early lunchers probably.

I got out, locked the car, and walked in.

"Hey Talia! I didn't know you were working today," One of the waiters, Stevie, called out. He had always been lovely to me.

"I'm not. I was just looking for Kylie. Do you know if she's around?"

Stevie frowned. "Not sure. Do you have her number?"

"I did, but I lost my cell, and I have to buy a new one."

Stevie pulled his phone out of his pocket, hit a few buttons, then handed me the phone.

I put it to my ear.

"Hello?" Kylie said in her sing-song voice.

"Kylie! It's Talia. I came to the restaurant looking for you, but Stevie decided calling you would be best." I grinned at the waiter as he went back to the register.

Kylie laughed. "Yeah, he's practical like that. What's up, Hun?"

"I, ah, need a place to stay tonight. I'm leaving tomorrow and was hoping I could stay with you for just one night."

I needed to organize some bank stuff, and mentally, I wasn't quite ready to haul ass across the state. I was shaky on my legs and still feeling stunned.

I wasn't sure I'd make it in my current state. I needed rest, and food.

"Of course, but what do you mean you're leaving? Aren't you getting married, like... next weekend?"

I rubbed the ring finger on my left hand, where my engagement ring used to rest. I'd put it into the jeweler a few days ago to have it cleaned, to make sure it sparkled for my big day.

I hadn't picked it up again, though I probably should. I could pawn it... maybe.

I put a hand to my head. "I'll explain later. Can I have your address again? I lost my cell, so I'm kinda a mess without it."

She laughed, told me the address, and we hung up.

"You okay getting there?" Stevie asked.

"Yeah, I've got a pretty good sense of direction."

Like most shifters, I had a good memory, and could find my way pretty much anywhere.

It also helped that Kylie only lived a couple of blocks from the restaurant.

I waved at him. "Thanks, Stevie."

"Anytime."

I got back into Dad's car, and before I knew it, I was sitting on Kylie's couch with a mug of hot chocolate and a warm blanket over my lap.

"Tell me everything," Kylie said, leaning forward in her chair, clearly wanting all the gossip.

I gave her a wan smile, and then concocted a humanized version of everything that had happened—which pretty much meant I had to lie about a lot. Kylie didn't know I was a wolf-shifter. Like most humans, she lived in blissful ignorance of the paranormal world around her.

At the end of my story, Kylie's mouth had dropped into a comical 'O', but her eyes were sympathetic.

"I'm so sorry to hear your dad passed, Talia. You must be devastated. Did you know he had heart issues?"

I shook my head, feeling slightly guilty about the lie. "It was sudden and unexpected."

"And then Maddox dropping you like a hot potato at the same time? Oh, honey, I can't even imagine what you've been through. I'm so sorry."

Her supportive words almost started another flood of tears, but I swallowed down the grief and concentrated hard to avoid crying. If I began again, I likely wouldn't be able to stop.

"You said that Maddox and you were, like, meant to be. Arranged since birth, yeah?"

I nodded. There was no such thing as fated mates in the human world, so I'd explained it to Kylie that Maddox and I were an arranged marriage.

My town was closed to outsiders, like most wolf-shifter towns. Kylie had never been there, and she had often expressed the thought—in an almost-joking sort of way—that we were some sort of cult, or something.

I shrugged. "It's all forfeited now. His family told me to get out of the state, or else."

Kylie frowned at me. "What do you mean, or else? They wouldn't hurt you or anything, would they?"

Of course, they would.

"No, I don't think so," I lied. "But rules are rules. And I have to go."

Kylie bit her lip. "Where to?"

I took a sip of the hot chocolate, grateful for the sweetness that washed away the bitter taste in my mouth.

"I don't actually know."

"Do you have any family, any friends? Anyone you could turn to?"

I thought about it for a minute, then realized there was one family member still living, and I hadn't even thought of her.

"There is, actually. A distant aunt. My mom's auntie, I think. She lives in Kansas. Wichita, I think."

Kylie whistled. "That's about a ten-hour drive from here."

I nodded. "I can do that in a day."

If I left by lunchtime tomorrow and didn't stop much, I'd be over the border in five hours or so, and another five hours to Wichita. That left me about twelve hours of wiggle room, or more.

"Do you have her number?" Kylie asked, grabbing her cell phone and sliding it over to me.

"I don't have it on me… But give me a sec. It could be in the car. I grabbed an address book before I left."

I ran outside, grabbed the box of things I'd gotten from Dad's room, and walked back inside. As suspected, there was his old-fashioned address book among the other documents and personal effects.

I flicked through the black leather book and found Aunt Sylvia's details.

"Thank God for my parents being the type of people who wrote everything down," I joked.

Kylie handed me her phone. "Yeah, I'd be screwed without my cell."

I moved into another room and called Sylvia. I hadn't seen her since I was very young, and in fact, could barely remember her to be honest. Our chat was brief, but it gave me hope. She was happy to help, and said I could live with her for as long as I wanted.

Relief swept through me. I had a place to run to, where before I had nothing, and now I could begin to make plans for the future.

When I walked back into the room, Kylie was pouring chips into a bowl, and had candies and chocolates in another.

When I raised a questioning eyebrow at her, she shrugged. "Hey, you've just been through hell losing your dad, you've broken up with your guy—who should have hung around to support you, the asshole—and I probably won't see you for ages, from the sound of it. Unless I want to visit you in Wichita. I don't see why we can't pig out and have a major calorie fest before you leave."

I grinned at her. As a wolf shifter, calories weren't something I worried about. We burnt off so much energy, our metabolism just wasn't comparable to the human kind. "Sounds perfect, Kylie. I really appreciate your support."

"That's what friends are for."

I sat down on the couch and reached for a handful of M&M's. I would miss Kylie when I left.

"Is there anything you need to do before you leave tomorrow?" Kylie asked as she walked into the kitchen, then came back with bottles of wine, one white and one red. "Which do you prefer?"

I groaned. After my hen's night, I didn't think I could stomach another drink. Not this year. "Neither, but I would love a soda."

"I've got heaps."

Kylie disappeared again, and came back with an assortment, and loaf of cheesy bread. "Wanna watch a movie?"

I nodded. "Sure." Anything that would take my mind off what had happened would be a blessing.

She found a chick flick that I knew would make me cry, and I shook my head. "Actually, can we do something with action? Not sure I can cope with a romantic comedy."

Kylie grinned, turned on *Kill Bill*, and we settled into the couch.

I stared at the screen. Perfect. Blood, and guts, and revenge. At least I wouldn't cry.

"Oh, you didn't answer me before. Is there anything you need to do before you leave?"

I shrugged, picking up the bowl of chips and plonking it in my lap. I was going to eat until I was sick. "I don't know. Maybe organize some money; bank stuff."

I had savings, and Dad did, too. He'd linked our accounts years ago.

He had said it was to help me with money management, but looking back, he'd obviously thought ahead, especially since he'd given me access to his accounts. Had he known something like this might happen one day? Had he suspected that I would be kicked out of the pack altogether, for his transgression?

"Do you need clothes? Food? Anything like that?"

I shook my head. "Nope. All good in that regard."

I think...

She nodded. "Then we relax here for the rest of the day, get an early night, and head to the shops in the morning."

I sighed. "That sounds like a great plan."

"I've got a huge bathtub here too, if you wanna soak? That always makes me feel better after a bad day."

I glanced over at my only human friend and sent up prayers of thanks for her. "That's exactly what I need. Thank you."

I spent the rest of the day eating myself into a food coma and fighting off the ebbs and flows of depression that ate at my resolve. I had a long hot bubble bath, then crawled into bed in Kylie's guest bedroom.

Part of me knew that I should have already been in the car and driving across state lines to get away from Maddox and his dad while I still had time. But I needed this night more than anything. It was a great reprieve from the stress of the last few days. I needed the moment to recoup my strength, and prepare for the next few days of travel.

I sighed and stared up at the ceiling. Travel? Who was I kidding? I was running away. Escaping the pack I had called family only days before.

Everything was turning out completely different to what I'd planned for my future.

My life wasn't meant to be headed this way. Since I'd turned eighteen and the Alpha's son had felt a mating bond with me, my life had been blessed.

Now, I was in the seventh ring of hell.

Alone.

Orphaned.

Abandoned.

Rejected.

And soon to be hunted.

At least I had a place to run tomorrow. Family to call on, even if it was a distant relative I barely remembered.

But it was a start. The beginning to a new life I'd never asked for, wanted, or expected.

What would Maddox do now? Forge another mating bond? Was that possible? Our mating bond hadn't been consummated, after all. Did that change things? Or would we both be destined to mourn each other forever? Would Maddox mourn me until the day he died?

I snorted at the thought. Not likely. Maddox was the Alpha's son. He was a soldier, doing whatever his father wanted. And he had made it clear through his rejection of me, that he was not there for me. He had shown the world—at least, the shifter world—that I was not his number one priority, mated bond or not.

I'd always thought of him as being loyal to his father, and the pack. But he'd abandoned me in my moment of need, so what did that make him? Certainly not loyal to me, the woman meant to be his wife.

The word *coward* circled in my mind, but I couldn't say it aloud. My love for Maddox still ran deep, as deep as my current feelings of betrayal.

I rolled over, nestled under the warmth of Kylie's blankets, and quietly cried myself to sleep.

THE NEXT DAY, I DRAGGED my depressed butt out of bed, then managed to drink a strong coffee before Kylie got me to drive her to the shops.

If I was honest with myself, I probably wouldn't have gotten out of bed if it wasn't for her. I would have stayed there and counted the minutes until the Alpha or his minions came for me. Would they really kill me?

"Thanks for the lift," Kylie said as we got out of my dad's car outside the restaurant where we worked. "I suppose I'll tell the boss you won't be doing any more shifts?"

I rounded the car. "Yeah... unfortunately." I rocked on the balls of my feet. "Thank you for yesterday, Kylie. I needed that day so badly. Things have just been so crazy."

I ran both hands through my bedraggled hair and Kylie pulled me in for a tight hug. "I'm gonna miss you."

I closed my eyes and hugged her back, enjoying her warmth and taking comfort from the friendship she was offering. "I'm gonna miss you too."

When I pulled back, I had tears in my eyes. I wasn't just moving away from the pack, but from my job, my friends, and everything I had ever known. Everything familiar.

Kylie glanced at her cell phone. "I better get inside. I'm gonna be late."

I gave her one more quick hug. "You go, I'll get all my errands done, then head for the border."

"Drive safe."

I nodded. "I will. Thanks, Hun."

Then I headed toward the bank, hurrying past two people I didn't know to stand on the edge of the street. I waited for the lights to change so I could walk across and go to the bank.

I was knocked sideways, almost into the road, and staggered before righting myself. I whirled to see who had bumped into me.

Two guys from my pack—well, my *former* pack—turned and glared at me before continuing on.

I rubbed my arm, which ached from the hit, and stood in my spot, staring at the bank across the street.

My pack had turned on me. It clear that I was no longer welcome in this town. I needed to get out as soon as possible.

I raced across the road as soon as the light turned green.

Out of the corner of my eye I spotted Shelly, a friend of my dad's.

I raised my hand to wave, and opened my mouth to call out to her.

Shelly lifted her hand to wave back, but her husband grabbed her arm and tugged her around to face away from me. They both walked away.

Shelly cast an apologetic look over her shoulder as they left, but didn't fight her mate when he dragged her away.

I pulled my shoulder bag closer to my body and hurried to the bank. I'd thought town was a neutral zone, where all shifters and humans could cohabitate without fear of a fight breaking out.

Obviously not.

I pushed open the door to the bank and went straight up to the teller. I pulled out all my IDs and said, "I'm moving interstate and need help transferring money around, please. And I need to pull out some cash, too."

I didn't take out as much money as I'd originally planned. Celia, God love her, had filled my glove box with cash, so I'd be right for a while, as long as I didn't need to purchase an apartment, or something big, straight away.

When I walked out of the bank, I took a deep breath of fresh air in through my nose and soaked in the warm sunshine on my face.

Life may have thrown me lemons—hell, it had cut my throat and shoved lemons into the wound—but I was alive. I had a chance of surviving all of this.

I would grab some brunch from the café and be on my way. It was only a five-hour drive to the border, then five to my aunt's house.

Then, and only then, would I be safe from the pack I had formerly called family.

GALEN

I stared at the superb-looking woman standing on the footpath outside the bank. She had her eyes closed, her head tilted up, and the wind was in her hair. She looked like some beautiful goddess, pausing in our town to drink in the humanity around her.

"Is that who I think it is?" I asked Tommy, staring at the woman across the street.

When she opened her eyes and a small, almost wistful smile lifted her lips, I almost sucked in a breath. That smile only made her more beautiful.

Lust kicked me in the groin, and I clenched my teeth in annoyance at my lack of self-control.

Get it together.

Tommy sidled up next to me. "Who? That chick over there? The blonde one?"

I nodded, following her with my eyes as she walked down the street and opened the door to one of the only good cafes in this town.

"Yeah, isn't she Maddox's girl?" Tommy asked. "Weren't they getting married or something?"

I nodded. "Yeah. That's her, all right."

I'd only seen her from a distance in the past, holding Maddox's arm and laughing up at him. The same kick in the gut had happened then, too, but I had successfully ignored it. Mostly.

A plan was forming in my mind. I had to think about the best possible way to avenge my fallen pack members, following the latest attack. And taking the next Alpha's mate, a key piece in the structure and hierarchy of their pack, was a perfect way to do it without further bloodshed.

I clapped my hands together. "I think I have an idea. But we need to follow her."

Tommy didn't question me as I jumped in my car, turned the key, and stared out the windshield at the woman.

How old could she be? Twenty? Twenty-one? Maybe a little older.

Something twanged in my chest as I watched her look left and right, then run across the road to jump into an old car.

I rubbed the spot on my ribs that ached in a foreign way, then pulled my car out of its park and followed her at a distance.

What was that strange feeling in my chest? Jealousy? It couldn't be.

There's no way I would ever be jealous of that coward, Maddox.

I glanced across the car at Tommy, who always kept his ear to the ground and knew more about the packs around us than anyone. "How much do you know about this chick and the next Alpha? Is it a love match? Or a power match?"

Sometimes, wolf packs did their version of an arranged marriage, putting the Alpha with the strongest or most powerful of the women. The girl I was following looked quiet and not at all tough, but looks were often deceiving.

"They say it's a love match," Noah said from the backseat, and my stomach dipped again. "Fated mates, actually, if what I heard in the pub last week was right."

She was *fated* to that loser? This time, the burning in my chest was unmistakable. Yep. Jealous as a wolf watching the full moon rise through the thick glass of a cage.

I wanted a mate. A wife. A woman who I could come home to, love, and protect. Who'd have my babies, and guard them with the fierceness of a wolf-shifting mother.

Sure, I'd been in no rush to find her in recent years, and no one was pushing me into mating someone I didn't want, which I was grateful for.

But a fated mate connection? A true love match? Just like my parents before me. I secretly wished for that. I wanted an equal partnership. One built on love, trust, and preferably the perfection of being touched by Fate.

The girl was likely heading back toward her pack grounds, based on the direction she was driving, and I shuddered. "She's driving home."

"What do you want to do?" Tommy asked me.

Whatever we did, the decision had to be made quickly. We couldn't just drive onto her lands. That would be suicide for all of us. The packs in this area had rules about boundary lines. Town was a neutral zone, and a peaceful area. Even if we were at war, the fight wasn't allowed to spill into the town where the humans were.

And if we ventured onto each other's territory without a direct invitation, it was war.

"I'm going to follow her," I said. "On foot. I'll try to intercept her before she reaches their land, or at least, not too far in from the boundary. You drive my car home and I'll meet you back there in a few hours."

I pulled over the car and opened the door.

Tommy grabbed my arm. "If they find you, you know you're as good as dead."

I rolled my eyes at him. I was one of the fastest in our pack, when in shifter form. "They'll have to catch me first."

I jumped out of the car, ripped off my shirt and jeans, and threw them in the back seat so I didn't ruin them.

Maddox's mate was getting further and further away. "Go, Tommy. Before they sense you. I won't be long."

If I all went according to the quickly formulated plan in my head, and with a bit of luck thrown in too,, I'd be bringing home the girl with me.

"Galen..."

I ignored Tommy's protest and let my shifter take over my body. I would need to run fast to catch her now.

As soon as my wolf paws hit the ground, I was moving. I darted off the road and wove my way through the trees, following the soft puff of smoke that trailed behind the old car but cutting through woodland area in a shortcut that would bring me close to the road further ahead.

My heart was pounding. Being so close to an enemy pack's territory, and contemplating snatching the mate of the Alpha's son—especially when we were currently at war with said pack—was dangerous.

Very. My father would have my head, if he ever found out.

But this was a gift horse we couldn't afford to ignore.

The girl was leverage and payback all rolled up into one.

I kept following her. As we hit edge of her pack's town, the girl didn't turn in to drive down the main strip of road like I'd expected her to. Instead, she veered around the town's outskirts and kept driving.

Where was she going?

My heart hammered hard as fear prickled along my veins. I needed to turn back. If they caught even a whiff of my scent this close, it would turn them rabid. This was dangerous, but God, I wanted to take them all down so badly. How stupid had they been to think they could just stroll onto our land and kill enough of us to take over the whole pack?

My father might be ill, but the rest of the pack remained strong and steadfast.

I kept running, veering around the pack grounds, keeping to the trees and trying not to be caught by anyone who might pose a threat to me.

I didn't think anyone in this pack had the balls to kill me, nor the strength now that we'd killed a dozen of their men. But without another heir, and with my father so sick, I was the only Alpha my pack had. They'd be lost without a leader.

And I might be skating on thin ice chasing after Maddox's mate but I damn sure wasn't going to let them catch me.

I would survive this, and more than that, I would make sure no one took my pack from me. No matter what I had to do.

Chapter 8

Talia

I pulled up my car next to the burial ground on my pack's land and turned off the engine. The smell of the chicken sandwiches beside me were making my mouth water, but I was saving them for the trip.

Back in town I'd gotten in the car with my fresh food, my new bank account details, and some cash, and then it hit me. Once I left, I'd never be able to visit my mother's gravesite again. Nor would I get to say a proper goodbye to my father.

Damn that idea to hell.

Tears threatened again, but instead, I'd pulled up my big girl panties, ignored all my instincts that told me returning to the pack was too dangerous, and drove straight here to the burial ground and my mother's grave.

I still had twenty-four hours. They could shun me, bump me, and ignore me all they liked. But they couldn't stop me from seeing my parents one more time. I had as much right to be here as any of them.

I stepped out of the car, shut the door, and pocketed the keys.

"Okay. I can do this," I said to myself, then I took a big deep breath and walked over to where the pack had buried my parents.

My father's plot was still covered in freshly turned soil. But there were still no flowers to decorate the site, and no gravestone to mark the final resting place of the man I'd loved. And unfortunately, I didn't expect there ever would be.

I knelt in front of my parents and tried to smile. "I'm going to miss you both so much."

I didn't want to be all choked up and unable to speak. I needed to get this out. To be able to say my final goodbyes properly. I swallowed hard and took a fortifying breath.

"I contacted Aunt Sylvia, and she seemed excited to have me stay with her. It'll be a whole new start. A new life, in a new town, a new state, maybe a new pack... I'm not sure what sort of life Aunt Sylvia lives. Human, or shifter. I don't really care. I just..."

I wiped my nose with my sleeve.

Kneeling here, I could almost feel my dad's grief, his regret at how everything had turned out. I turned my gaze to stare at where my father's body lay buried beneath the earth. "I'm so sorry I couldn't do more to help you, Dad. I should have known... Maddox should have told me... I'm so..."

I couldn't get the final sorry out. My throat closed up and there was no talking.

I love you, Dad.

I turned to my mother and tried to speak, but there was nothing I could say or do to get the words out.

I gave up and spoke to her inside my head, where the prayers went.

Mom. I love you. And I am so, so sorry I didn't take better care of Dad for you. I tried... I promise I tried. But I wasn't good enough to keep him... from this.

I began to sob as the thoughts poured through me, and even though part of me wanted to stay there forever, I knew I couldn't.

I pushed my hands into the cold earth and staggered to my unsteady feet. I glanced up at the clear blue sky and blinked rapidly.

"I need to go. The pack have orders to hunt me down if I'm still here come morning, so I'd better..." I motioned to the old car that stood behind me. "I hope I get to come back one day. But I... who knows?"

I clenched my hands into tight fists and willed the despair away.

This was my last chance to say what I needed to. I just had to concentrate hard enough to stop the sobbing.

I took several breaths, in and out, forcing the tears back, and the bile down.

Finally, I opened my eyes and stared at the place my parents both rested.

"I love you both. So much. Thank you for being my parents. I promise to try and do you proud. Bye for now..."

And with my head held high, I managed to walk away without shedding another tear.

I wasn't staying here to be killed like my father had been. I'd lost my parents, my husband and the man who had been my mate, but I hadn't lost my life. Not yet anyway.

I got back in the car and wiped my hands off on a wipe, then reached for my chicken sandwich. The first bite was pure bliss, and the second was better. By the third I was feeling a little more normal. My stomach was growling, but there was now a sense of peace to my body.

My shoulders relaxed, crawling down from the place up near my ears.

I glanced out my windshield at the clear sky and open landscape. I was about to drive across the state line for the first time ever.

The unknown awaited.

I quickly ate the rest of my sandwich and turned the key. Shit. I needed gas, and then I could leave. There was a gas station on the highway, between the two pack's lands.

As far as I knew, it was a neutral zone.

Maddox had never let me visit there, but he wasn't running my life anymore.

I could do anything I wanted. It was such a strange feeling.

I drove to the small station, filled up my dad's car, and set off. It was two hundred miles to the border. I should make it on this tank, but if I didn't, surely there'd be another place to get gas somewhere on the highway.

The fact that I didn't know that kind of thing freaked me out. I hadn't realized how sheltered a life I had led, being looked after by Dad and "managed" by Maddox. But, I was too far gone now to turn around.

I took a back track and turned onto a dirt road, looking for signs to the highway, slowing down to peer out the window.

I slammed on the brakes as a huge black wolf jumped onto the road in front of me. My car fishtailed and swerved.

Panic wove through me as the car stalled.

"Come on. Come on." I twisted the key over and over, but the car wouldn't turn over.

Then the black wolf transformed into a huge man with long hair to his shoulders, and the largest body I'd ever seen.

Huge, hulking shoulders, massive thighs…

He skulked toward me, ripped open my car door, and reached over me to unfasten my seat belt. All before I had moved a muscle.

I was frozen in place, shocked into silence by his sudden appearance, and by the sheer enormity of his superbly proportioned body.

He grabbed me by the wrists and wrenched me out of the car.

"What are you doing?" I choked out the words as I stared up into his dark eyes.

He still looked feral, which some men did after shifting back from their wolf forms. The animal was still inside him, larger than life and pushing hard to get out.

"You're Maddox's mate." The words were hard to make out around the sharp teeth still present in his mouth.

How did he know who I was? As far as I knew, I had never seen this man before.

He shook me, and my teeth practically rattled in my head.

"Yes! Yes. I'm Talia," I squeaked out. I was still processing that I wasn't Maddox's mate anymore. And in this moment, when the enormous man had pulled me out of the car, I wasn't thinking straight.

Was he looking specifically for me? Was he going to hurt me? He wasn't a shifter from our pack, but what if he'd been hired by the Alpha to track me down, and kill me?

Fear rushed through my veins. I could feel my shifter rising inside me. I wasn't a good fighter, but I was fast. Could I get away from this guy? I wasn't sure. But if it came down to my life, then I'd fight with everything I had.

"You're coming with me," he said, grabbing tighter to one wrist and pulling me off the highway and into the forest.

He almost yanked me off my feet he was so strong.

I glanced back at my dad's old car and tried to plant my feet, tugging in the opposite direction to where he was dragging me. I couldn't stop him, but I did manage to slow him down a touch.

"My car! Everything I own is in that car. Please."

He grunted like he hadn't heard me and I yanked my arm back, fighting hard to turn around. When I managed to pull my arm out of his grip, I pivoted on one foot and tried to make a run for it.

I made it one step before he grabbed me around the waist and threw me over his shoulder like I weighed less than a bag of flour.

I cried out, pounding my fists against his back. "Please! I can't leave the car there! Please!"

My money! My clothes! Everything that was important to me was in that car. It was all I had left of my life. All I had left of the connection with my dad.

He stopped walking as though he was considering my plea. There wasn't a sound around us. Not even a bird chirping.

All I could hear was the pounding of my heart in my ears.

"You got the keys?" he demanded.

I shook my head. "No. They're in the ignition."

I hadn't even had time to pull them out.

He grunted dismissively. "No problem. I'll send someone back for it. Only *my* pack uses these back roads. They're on our land."

My pack. Our land. Who was this guy? Was he an Alpha, too, like Maddox's dad?

"Fuck it." I let go of the fight, relaxing against his back to conserve my energy. No wonder why Maddox had always told me not to go to the gas station in town.

It was theirs? A neighboring pack?

He could have explained that, and I've have given it a wide berth.

The big and very naked shifter walked for so long I began to get numb and tingly in my hands. I was just about to say something to the guy, when there were shouts and men came running toward us.

Had we reached their pack town? I tried to lift up and turn around so I could see who was there, but my captor just used his other hand to push me down. "Stay there."

I groaned, but didn't fight him. What was I going to do if he put me down anyway? Run away from a rival pack group of super fit men?

I was dead. Clearly, it was only a matter of time as to when.

"Markus. Go get her car and bring it here. Don't touch any of her stuff. It's on Dawsons Road, a mile out from the gas station."

"Will do."

Relief flooded through me. He'd asked them not to touch my stuff.

I was being kidnapped, probably to use against my old pack and Maddox. But that small amount of understanding and thoughtfulness about my belongings made tears prickle at the backs of my eyes. He listened. He cared.

I hung my head in shame.

God, you really have stooped to a new level of low if you're happy at the tiniest bit of kindness thrown your way from a kidnapper.

"I'm gonna throw her in the shed. Make sure everyone knows to stay away," the kidnapper said, and my ears pricked up.

He was gonna do... what?

Then my big naked abductor sauntered away from the others and back into the forest, with me still draped over his shoulder.

I glanced up as we walked away. The pack guys he'd been talking to still stood around in a small group, watching us. I gave up caring what anyone thought. This was pretty much as undignified a position as one could get, but at least no one was laughing at me, or pushing and shoving me into the road.

Like my own packmates. *Former*, I reminded myself.

The concerned looks on these men's faces as the big guy carried me off were obvious.

They were about my age, probably a bit older.

What was this guy's plan?

We continued on in silence until the pack was long out of sight. I zoned out, trying not to think too much. There wasn't much I could do, like this.

Eventually, my captor lowered his shoulder, and I fell onto my ass on a hard wood patio.

"Ow," I said, rubbing my tingling hands and staring up at the still naked man before me.

Holy shit he was big. Everywhere. I averted my gaze from the part that was just about eye height right now.

"Get inside," he demanded, and I shivered at the sound of his voice.

Damn, if he's not an Alpha, I'll bite my own ass.

He must be the Alpha of this pack, whatever it was.

But what the hell was an Alpha doing kidnapping me?

I pushed to my feet, my legs trembling. "What are you going to do with me?"

He grinned as though he had all the time in the world, and crossed his beefy arms over his even beefier chest. "I don't know yet. But I can tell you that you better get that ass inside, or..."

I was running for the log cabin before he even finished the sentence.

As a virgin, I had an insane amount of fear wrapped around the first time I would have sex. I'd always assumed it would be with Maddox, on our wedding night. That dream was now in tatters, but that didn't mean I had to submit to the nightmare of being taken by force by a stranger who would never understand how terrified I was.

I pulled open the door and raced over the threshold, a tingle of awareness shooting up my spine as I stumbled into the house.

"Oh, no." I knew that feeling.

Magic.

The place must be warded.

I stumbled around, crashing into a bookcase, then a couch, before finally falling to my knees on a worn rug.

The magic was knocking me out.

I lifted my head and stared at the naked Alpha looming over me. Dark spots danced at the edge of my sight, and my brain was beginning to shut down.

"Please don't hurt me," I whispered, fighting against the magic of whatever sort of spell had been woven into the door of this place.

He frowned as though he didn't understand why I was struggling. Could he not feel it? The magic was strong, so strong. But I needed to be clear with my words, so there would be no mistake.

"I'm a virgin... please... don't..."

I couldn't fight the effect of the magic anymore.

I fell toward the floor, and everything went black.

Chapter 9

Galen

She was a virgin?

God, no...

I dove forward to catch her before her head smashed against the ground, tangling my fingers in the long red and gold strands of her hair just in time.

"Fucking hell," I muttered as I lowered her unconscious form to the rug, then gathered her up again in my arms.

What sort of Alpha would leave a woman like this... his mate... untouched?

"A fucking idiot, that's who," I answered my own question.

I walked the rival Alpha's soon-to-be-wife into the bedroom and placed her gently on the bed.

Untouched... fuck. It was unheard of in this part of the woods. We took what was ours, and it was given willingly.

I shook my head and walked away, wishing I'd been able to tell the girl before she fainted that no one in this pack was going to rape her. Not unless they wanted their head placed on a fucking pike out the front.

This woman, who was barely more than a girl, had nothing to do with the fight I was having with her pack. I would keep her as a bargaining tool, sure. But I wouldn't hurt her, and neither would any of my men.

"Hey! Galen!" someone called from outside, but I found myself unwilling to leave her, which was insane. She wasn't mine to protect. She was my prisoner, the mate of the rival pack's next Alpha, and nothing to me. Then why was it so hard to walk out the front door and greet my Betas as if nothing was amiss?

I stared at the excited faces of David, Markus, and Theo.

"Did you do it? Did you really do it?" Theo asked, jumping up and down like a puppy.

I growled at him to calm down as I prowled off the step. I needed some clothes, but I didn't want to leave this place to go get them. "You guys brought spare jeans with you?"

They shook their heads.

Then Markus said, "I'll go get you some."

He trotted off.

"Be quick," I called, and watched him speed up.

He'd read me well, and that was something I needed in my lead beta. I hadn't formally chosen my men yet, or the council members I wanted to add from my generation when my father's time came to an end.

But I was always on the lookout for people who were loyal, clever, and good fighters.

All of which Markus was.

"So?" Theo asked again. "Is she here? Did you really kidnap their next Alpha's mate?"

I nodded. "I did. Her name is Talia, and none of you are to touch her. Do you understand?"

Theo frowned. "Why would we?"

David crossed his arms over his chest like he was offended. "As if."

I shook myself, trying to drag myself back to a base level of calm. She'd thrown me off, that girl. Maybe I shouldn't hang around until she woke up. I needed to get away from her, run off this tension.

I looked at David. "Because she's young, and scared, and she's not to be hurt. Can I leave you in charge of her while I go check on my dad?"

David walked up the steps that led into the cabin. "Yeah. You can trust us."

I nodded, fighting the need to growl at them the closer they got to her.

"Let me know when she's awake."

Theo frowned at me. "She's asleep? Seriously? Wow. She must have been pretty tired."

"Yeah. Magical sleep. I had one of the local witches put up wards around the cabin. If anyone that isn't of our pack steps over the threshold, they pass out. I hadn't expected it to work quite so well, or so quickly."

I frowned at the window that was off the bedroom I'd left Talia in. Hopefully she'd be okay.

"Clever," Theo said. "Great place to keep prisoners, and ensure they remain under control."

I didn't really want to think about how many people we may need to hole up there in the next few weeks, months, or years. Nor the fact that it would likely be me making those decisions in future, rather than my dad. So, I ignored his comment and turned to take the jeans from Markus, who had returned quickly as I requested.

"Thanks," I said, pulling them on, then took the gray tank from him with a grateful smile. "That's great."

I tugged on the shirt and clapped Markus on the back. "I'm going over to speak to Dad, then to the bar afterward if anyone needs me."

That should help me lose this strange feeling about the girl.

The virgin.

No. *Maddox's* girl, I reminded myself. Off-limits, for about a thousand different reasons.

I trotted down the hill and jogged through our town, my heart rate higher than it should be. I moved faster, wanting to burn off whatever excess energy this was. I ran the length of the pack grounds, then circled back, watching as Tommy drove Talia's old car through town, then parked it outside my dad's place.

I jogged up to him, a nice sweat covering my skin and cooling me down. "Thanks for doing that, Tommy."

He nodded at me. "Anytime."

He threw the keys at me and frowned.

"What's up?" I asked.

He shook his head. "I don't know. Something's weird about this. It looks like she's packed up to move away or something. There're pillows, clothes, blankets, photos, even cash in there. You sure she's the Alpha mate you think she is?"

She had confirmed it, and I was sure I'd seen her that one time hanging off Maddox's arm. But why she'd packed up her car for that sort of trip, I didn't know.

I shrugged. "No idea. I'll ask her when she wakes up."

I headed inside my dad' house. "Hey, Dad! You home?" I picked up a note left by a neighbor that said there was dinner in the fridge.

A chuckle came from the nearest bedroom. "No. I'm out running through the forest."

I smiled at the jest, but there was little humor in my heart. My father hadn't shifted in months, let alone gone for a run through the woods.

I pushed open the door to his room and walked inside. The smell struck me, hard. It smelled of decay, and a little of death.

"We need some fresh air in here, Dad," I said, trying to keep the tone light.

"I like it dark in here," Dad grumbled.

I ignored him, going over to the windows and pushing two of them open, while keeping the curtains drawn so it was still semi-dark.

"There. You'll breathe easier now," I said, before plopping down on the chair next to his bed. "How's your day been?"

He shrugged. "Same as most days, no worse. What's happened?" Dad narrowed his eagle eyes at me. "You look ... concerned."

I struggled not to laugh. That was my dad's word for worried and excited at the same time.

"I am concerned," I said. "I've taken a step to fulfil my promise to you. To stand up for our pack and avenge our fallen."

Dad pushed himself up in bed until he was sitting up and leaning against the headboard. "What have you done?"

I leaned back and grinned. "I spotted a girl in town."

"A girl? What sort of girl?"

"Maddox's girl," I said with a grin. "Their next Alpha's soon-to-be-mate."

My dad swallowed, his eyes gleaming with interest, but his tone was cautionary when he said, "The town's a neutral zone."

I nodded. "I know. So, I followed her, and when she drove back to her pack, I shifted into my wolf form and ran after her."

"Galen! You could have been killed."

I swiped my hand through the air, dismissing his worry. "She visited a graveyard. There was a freshly dug grave there, but no marker. Then afterward, she headed to the gas station to refuel."

My dad's eyes brows flew higher on his forehead. "Our gas station? That's not neutral ground."

I grinned. "I know. So I grabbed her, carried her back here, and threw her into the cabin, where the magic I had arranged to have instilled in the boundaries knocked her out."

My dad's mouth opened, but nothing came out.

I wanted to laugh, but instead, a shot of self-pride raced through me at his pleased expression. He was also shocked. That was a first.

"What are you going to do with her?" he finally asked.

I shrugged. "Not a hundred per cent sure, but we can definitely use her as leverage against the Northwood pack. I'm certain of it."

He nodded, glancing away. "Yes. It's a bold move, son."

I sighed. "I know, but I don't want any more blood spilt, if we can stop the war now. I figured that if we were smart, showed a united front and strength, her capture would get the others to back down. We can release her once they agree to that, and our show of good will in letting her go without harm should mean they can't easily attack again. Unless they want to lose face across all the packs in North America."

My father nodded slowly. "Yes. Though your plan hinges on the girl being valuable."

I grinned. "Why wouldn't she be? She's the fated mate of the Alpha's only son."

"Fated? Shit!" My dad's laugh was strong, and made the hairs on my arms stand on end.

That was the sound of my father from when I was younger, when he was fit and strong and able. I *loved* the sound of that laugh.

"You are one lucky man, Galen. But smart, too. That was a good call, son," he said with a grin, then began to cough.

And cough. And he didn't stop.

I jumped up to help but he waved me back. He coughed until blood stained his fist, and then he tried to wipe it away on his blankets.

"Dad! Your hand! It's…"

"I know," he said, the annoyance shining through even though he sounded hoarse.

He cleared his throat, threw back his head so that his hair cleared his eyes, and stared at me.

"Why do I feel like I'm in trouble?" I asked.

Dad shook his head. "You're not. I am."

I narrowed my eyes. "You're in trouble? What for?"

What could he have possibly done from his bed?

Dad sighed. "I think you need to publicly take over the role of Alpha."

My mouth gaped open. "That's just not done, Dad. Not..." I broke off, unable to finish. *Not yet. Not till you're dead.*

The role of Alpha passed from father to son, on the father's death. Not before. Unless a challenger came in to battle for the role, but that rarely happened. An Alpha was born the largest and strongest of our kind. Not many Beta wolves were strong enough to survive a battle against an Alpha. Not even if they teamed up.

Dad reached over and grabbed my hand, squeezing it tight. "You have to, Galen. Otherwise, if someone outside of the pack chooses to challenge me, I'll have to fight."

To the death.

"I would avenge you," I said, my wolf teeth cutting into my lower lip as I began a partial shift in anger.

My dad pressed his lips together and nodded once. "You must take the role now. To show strength in our pack."

I shook my head. "It isn't done, Dad."

"That's because Alpha's are never sick. We are strong, until we die in battle. Or old age. This sickness—whatever it is—is going to kill me, Galen. And I would rather my last memories be of my son rising to the role he was born for."

Tears and emotion clogged my throat as I stared down at my father. What was it, this illness that was killing him? If we could work out what it was, maybe he had a chance. But no one knew, not the shifters, nor the witches, nor anyone, it seemed.

Finally, I nodded. "Okay, Dad."

What else could I do? Deny the final wishes of a dying man?

Besides, like always, his request made sense. My father was the most sensible person I knew.

Dad lay back against his pillows, exhausted. "You will be a great Alpha, Galen. You love our people. You're strong and loyal. And you have a good moral compass."

I chuckled, brushing off the compliments. "Be careful, Dad. You'll blow my ego up too big and I won't fit through the door."

My dad shook his head. "Nothing wrong with being honest."

"True."

We sat that way for a while, in the quiet. In peace.

I'd originally had plans to head back into town and check on the bar, but instead I stayed with my dad and talked more about how I would take over officially, and how to plan a ceremony that in the history of our people, had never happened.

By the time we were done, the sun had dropped out of the sky and it was time for dinner. I heated something up for Dad from one of the dinners that had been dropped off by pack females, then glanced outside, where Markus was resting by the car Talia had been driving when I found her.

I handed Dad his lamb stew and cocked my head. "Markus is outside. I'm gonna go speak to him, then I'll be back."

Dad waved his hand. "Don't hurry back. You do have a life outside this sick old man."

I clenched my jaw in denial of his words, but without anything to say back, I just stomped over to the front door and opened it up.

"Hey Markus. Come in for a beer," I said.

God knew I needed one.

What a day.

I'd done my first kidnapping, and unfortunately it was the beautiful soon-to-be wife of my enemy. And I didn't even hate her enough to be mad at her. She'd looked so terrified when she'd seen me on the road.

A *virgin*? I shook my head. Was that idiot Maddox insane as well as stupid?

I groaned as I threw open the fridge and pulled out some drinks.

Now my father wanted me to take over as Alpha, years before I should.

"Here," I said, handing Markus the beer.

"Thanks." He gave a nod before he tipped the drink back.

"Any news?" I asked. "About the she-wolf in the cabin?"

Markus shrugged and leant against the counter. "Not really. She hasn't moved since last night."

I frowned. "She's not even awake yet?"

"Nope." Markus finished off his beer and sighed. "I'm gonna head home for some dinner. Theo said he'd do the night shift."

"I'll go talk to him."

I tossed my empty beer bottle in the recycling and headed up to the cabin. The night was quiet and cool, just as I liked it. I kept my ears open and my eyes wide, checking to see if our enemy was coming once again for us in the night.

I still couldn't believe the Northwood Alpha and his pack had thought to take me out. Or my father.

What the hell had they been thinking?

I trudged up the hill and waved to Theo, who was standing guard on the patio.

"You okay to stay here over night?" I asked him.

He nodded. "Yeah, no problem. I'll call you if she wakes up."

I wanted to stay here as well but that was stupid. Theo could watch her. She was just a prisoner after all.

There was only one thing. "Remember that there's safety on the other side of that door for you. If some of her pack come looking for her, just go inside and they'll pass out the moment they try to cross the threshold."

Theo saluted. "That's great. Thank you."

Despite the strange tug to stay, I turned and walked away. My dad needed me, and I would stay with him again tonight. I didn't know how much time I had left with him, which would kick me in the guts enough when he died, but the idea that I'd have to be Alpha soon was even harder.

How was I going to look after all my people, without my father at my side?

Chapter 10

Talia

When I opened my eyes, I was staring up at a ceiling I'd never seen before. It had white plaster, but low hanging rafters that reminded me of a log cabin.

But not mine.

I sat up and gasped, furtively looking around. This wasn't my pack's cabin. All the memories of being kidnapped came rushing back in. And then the rush of magic as I stepped through the door. It must have been warded, and knocked me out.

How long had I been unconscious? Had anyone...

Fear flooded me and I quickly checked my body for injuries, running my hands over my neck, my breasts, and legs. Nothing seemed sore, or ill-used. My clothing was all still in place.

Relief flooded me. I hadn't been touched. I'd know if I'd been hurt, or abused in some way.

A memory hit me, of a large black wolf shifter stopping me from driving out of town.

Shit! What time was it? My seventy-two hours might be almost up, or worse. I may have already run out of time altogether.

I jumped off the comfortable bed and raced to the window. I threw back the gray curtains and was blasted with sunshine. Judging by the position of the sun, it was at least the next day.

I raised my hand to shield my eyes. "Crap!" I said out loud. "I'll never make it over the state line now."

I had to try, though. What else could I do?

I raced to the bedroom door and pulled it open. The front door wasn't far. I stumbled over my feet trying to get there, another memory rising and confronting me. The shifter... the man... had carried me here. He'd promised he wouldn't hurt me.

Despite his size, and intimidating aura, he'd been... kind. For a kidnapper.

He'd obviously been true to his word, and not hurt me. So far.

But if I didn't get out of here soon, the kidnapper and his pack would be the least of worries. My own pack were going to hunt me down and kill me the way they'd killed my father.

I pulled open the front door, but the moment I tried to step over the threshold, an invisible force threw me back. I landed heavily on my ass.

Damn it. The ward was still in place. And it worked both ways, in and out of this cabin.

I rolled to the side to rub the offended spot on my rear.

A huge man with blond scruffy hair blocked the doorway. "You're finally awake."

He growled at me as though I'd done something wrong, laying about sleeping in and being lazy, even though I was the one being held prisoner and I'd had no choice about whether or not I was awake.

I jumped to my feet, my wolf shifter rising within me. "Why can't I get out of this cabin?"

The guy, who seemed younger than I first thought now that I was looking at him properly, quirked a smile at me. "It's warded. You can't get through."

"Well, obviously its warded. But I have to leave! You don't understand."

He frowned at me. "Why? Worried your boyfriend will miss you?"

I opened my mouth to tell him the truth, and then realized the only reason they'd captured and not killed me, was probably because they thought I was still Maddox's bride-to-be.

Tears clouded my vision, and I blinked them away.

I opened my mouth to respond, and the guy, who couldn't be much older than me, backed away. "You just stay there. I'll go get Galen."

Before I could reply, he hurried away.

I clenched my hands into fists and strode forward, bouncing back off the invisible shield again, like I'd smacked into something solid.

"Fuck!"

I ran my hands through my hair, frazzled at the entrapment. What the hell was I going to do now?

How would I ever manage to get away from this pack? Or my pack? It felt like the whole world was about to be on my tail even if I did manage to run.

On the other side of the living room, a huge window let in the morning sun. I bolted over to the window, threw open the pane, and felt a moment's excitement before I was forcefully pushed back against my will once more.

The windows, too?

"Shit!"

There was a knock at the open door, and a blond guy slid two plates along the floor toward me.

Food.

I walked back over to where the same young guy, with tousled hair and the beginnings of a beard, was staring at me like he'd never seen a girl before.

"What's your name?" I asked him as I picked up the plate with my sandwich on it. The same one I'd bought yesterday and taken a few bites out of.

I was so hungry I didn't care. The sandwich was stone-cold now, but it was still delicious.

"Galen's on his way," he said, not answering my question. He disappeared from view by walking along the patio so I could no longer see him.

Galen... was that the name of the Alpha who grabbed me yesterday?

I took another bite, chewing and swallowing despite the goosebumps of fear that covered my skin, and the tumultuous feelings rolling around in my belly. I was starving. How long had I been out for? Was it more than a day?

"Who's Galen?" I called out in between bites.

The guy stepped back into my line of view. "He's our Alpha's son."

I rolled my eyes. Of course, he was. I seemed to attract those assholes.

"Great."

The kid disappeared again, and I took my plate of sandwiches, and the extra plate of cookies he'd pushed into the room, over to the couch and sat down.

It was obvious I was in enemy pack land, being held captive. Although I could easily have let fear consume me, at this point, I didn't have a whole lot to lose.

They were feeding me and keeping me safe, overall, which was more than I could say for my own pack. But if I could convince the Alpha's son to let me go, I would jump in my car and hightail it straight over the border.

I finished my sandwich but couldn't bring myself to eat one of their cookies, even though they looked homemade, and delicious, with little chocolate chips throughout

I swallowed hard, my throat beginning to ache. I needed a drink.

I wandered over to the small kitchen, found a glass in one of the cupboards, and turned on the faucet.

Clean water flowed out, and I smiled as I filled my glass. So, they weren't complete barbarians after all.

"Making yourself at home?" a deep voice asked from behind me.

I sprayed a mouthful of the water I'd been drinking all over the cupboards in front of me, then slapped a hand over my mouth, trying to stop the rest coming out.

I swallowed hard and spun around to confront my kidnapper. "Don't sneak up on me like that."

His eyebrows flicked up, and I got my first good look at his face. I was sure I'd seen him in town at least once. Who could miss a guy towering over six foot six, and as big as a fridge? He had an air about him, too, that drew the eye and held it. He looked like he came from Alpha blood. There was something robust about him—beyond his size—that gave the distinct impression he was a leader of men.

But despite that air, and the hard set of his jaw, his eyes seemed kind.

I set down my glass and walked back over to the couch, sinking onto the cushions to assume a submissive position.

I didn't feel submissive right in this moment. Part of me wanted to punch him in those hard abs for daring to kidnap me. But I didn't want him thinking I was challenging him in any way. The best way to get out of here was to make him think I wasn't a threat. To him, or to anyone else from his pack.

He crossed his arms over his big meaty chest, his biceps bulging.

I swallowed. This was one Alpha who looked like he was strong enough to lead a whole pack of shifters. I couldn't help the quick thought that flickered into my head, comparing him to my now-ex-fiancé. Maddox didn't really like to exercise, or work out, and his father never made him do any physical labor because he knew his son didn't like it.

Maddox was lean and long, not heavily muscled. I'd always liked Maddox's slim body, but this guy was all male.

"What were you doing on our lands yesterday?"

"*Your* lands?" I squeaked as I repeated part of the question. "I was just filling up my car with gas, and driving home."

"You weren't driving home. Don't lie to me." He growled. "You were headed in the complete opposite direction to your pack, and town. So where were you going? With enough cash to buy a new car, and enough clothes and possessions to move house."

I blinked rapidly as tears pooled in my eyes. I had to come up with a good lie, and quickly.

Focusing on being kidnapped had actually helped me contain my grief, but this guy's questions brought it all rushing back. "My father died." I covered my mouth to stifle the sob that rose. It was still ridiculously hard to say out loud. "I decided to go visit my aunt. She lives in Wichita. She said I could stay with her for a while."

He narrowed his eyes. "What about your future husband? What did *he* have to say about that?"

"Maddox?" I repeated. I must have sounded stupid, to him, but my brain was slow in concocting a story.

He nodded. "Yes. Why would he let his future wife leave the state? Especially if you've just lost a parent. I wouldn't let you leave my side, if you were mine."

I blinked at him.

If you were mine.

Well, I'm not yours, I thought. I'm not anybody's, anymore.

His words made me realize that no one outside our pack knew what had happened to my father and myself.

I frowned at him. "Is this about Maddox? Did you kidnap me to get to him?"

He didn't answer, but I saw the truth in his eyes.

Now I really couldn't tell him Maddox had rejected our bond. I'd have nothing to bargain with if they planned to use me against him. Hopefully, when they did inevitably find out, they wouldn't kill me and toss my body over the pack lines just to prove a point.

"Answer my question," he said.

I stood up, not because I really wanted to, but something told me to get on my feet. I wouldn't die on the ground, like a dog.

"Maddox told me to take some time to mourn my father. He loves me." I stuck my nose in the air, though it took everything in me to lie like that.

Galen, if that was his name, glared at me. "Were you part of the hunting party that killed two of my men?"

My mouth dropped open. "Your men... Oh, my God, you're the pack they attacked..."

That's what this is all about!

When the big Alpha took an aggressive step forward, I held up both of my hands and took retreating steps back. "No! Of course not! Women in my pack aren't allowed to fight. That's men's business."

"Where were you when it was all happening then?" he countered.

I narrowed my gaze at him. "If you really must know, I was in bed with a hangover from my bachelorette party the night before."

His mouth practically fell open, before he turned and marched away.

He obviously hadn't been expecting that response.

When he reached the door, he turned around and glared at me. "Your pack will pay for what they did to my men."

"What's that got to do with me?" I demanded. "I wasn't even there."

"Your Alpha ordered the attack, and your 'fated mate,'" he said, as though the term disgusted him, "will pay for his part in it as well."

I was in the middle of something bigger than I had realized. I began to sob as I ran to the door after him. "Please. Just let me go. I won't tell Maddox you grabbed me. I'll just drive to Wichita to be with my aunt. She's expecting me."

He turned to look at me from the fresh air outside the cabin. "You'll stay my prisoner until I've come up with a plan to use you against your pack."

"But..."

He waited, but I didn't have anything else to say. How could I tell him that it wouldn't work? That my pack didn't want me anymore? In fact, if he killed me, he'd be doing them a favor. They had orders to kill me on sight.

"Please..."

Another guy came running up, bounced up the stairs, and whispered in the Alpha's ear, before bounding off again.

Galen speared me with a wordless look, one I couldn't read, and then without saying another thing, the huge shifter man turned and ran after the other man, disappearing from sight.

Chapter 11

Galen

Fucking hell. Dad had been taken to hospital in town, which could only mean one thing. He'd gotten so bad one of his neighbors must have called the paramedics.

That wasn't a good sign.

I ran until I reached my truck which was parked outside Dad's place, jumped in, and took off. "Damn it," I fumed out loud, even though there was no one to hear me. "He was okay last night."

I'd been working out when they came to tell me Talia was awake this morning. I'd been out for over an hour, and I hadn't thought to check on Dad before I went to the cabin to see Talia. He'd still been asleep when I got up.

I drove way over the speed limit and didn't care, reaching the small hospital in less than ten minutes.

I swung my vehicle into the closest parking spot and ran inside. When I found my dad, he was in an ICU room, hooked up to a myriad of beeping machines and an oxygen mask covering his face.

"Are you family?" a nearby nurse asked.

I nodded, swallowing the lump in my throat. "I'm his son."

She directed me to a chair next to his bed and said, "A doctor should be along soon." The sympathy in her words only added to my anxiety.

I waited, nervous energy engulfing me.

The staff were jittery, as humans always were around wolf shifters, and they were confused by the lack of records in relation to my dad.

"He's never really been sick before," I said.

The next few hours were terrible. I sat in the room that smelled of detergent and dying people and watched my father's chest rise and fall. At least the machines were keeping his breathing relatively even.

He didn't wake up and no doctors came to check on him in the time I sat there.

Eventually, I had to leave.

I got up and turned to go, only to run into a gray-haired doctor, with glasses sliding off his nose.

"Finally," I said, and he stared at me with wide eyes. There may have been a touch too much growl in my tone. I took a deep breath and released it slowly.

He extended his hand. "Doctor Michaels."

"Galen," I said, pulling my frustration in by the reins. "This is my father."

"Incredible case," the doctor said. "He has no medical history in this hospital whatsoever."

I wanted to roll my eyes. Of course, he didn't. Wolf shifters didn't get sick. Not that the doctor knew he was a shifter, of course.

"I explained to the other staff that he's always been well. He's never been here before, because he has never needed to be here."

"When did this start?" the doctor asked, and we got into a history of my father's mystery illness.

In the end, the doctor offered to run what sounded like a hundred tests, and promised he'd contact me as soon as he knew more.

Despite the tardiness of his arrival, he seemed to be competent, and I relaxed a touch, leaving my dad in this human doctor's relatively capable hands.

"Where can I leave my number?" I asked him. The doctor directed me back to the nurse's station.

I wrote down my details on the papers they shoved at me. "I'm only ten minutes away, so please call me when he wakes up."

"Of course," the nurse replied, though I got the feeling she wasn't certain he would wake up at all.

When I headed out of the hospital's parking lot, the sun had passed the highest point in the sky, and was well on its way down.

I ran a hand through my hair.

How many hours have I been sitting in that chair?

I pulled my cell phone out of my pocket and checked the time.

"*Jeez.* Three o'clock already."

I swung past the bakery for a couple of hot pies and headed back out of town again.

I didn't see any of the enemy pack members in town, but the situation with Dad occupied my mind, so I wasn't really looking. It was the one great thing about the treaty we all held tight to, safety within town. Our own pack borders couldn't be crossed without outright war, but the main town was a green zone.

Had we gotten into fights over the years? Hell yes.

At my bar? Often.

But no one had been killed in town in my lifetime, and I hoped it never got to that. There were laws that all shifters abided by when it came to humans, and leaving them in their ignorance was one of them. If we turned our quiet little town into an all-out turf war, there would be hell to pay.

I drove straight back to the cabin where Talia was being kept. I wanted to make sure the wards still held, and that she wasn't making a nuisance of herself.

I pulled up in front of the cabin and got out of the truck. I had competent staff looking after the bar for me at the moment, so I planned to drive back into town after this and sleep in my own bed rather than head back to work. I was closer to the hospital that way.

Markus was sitting on the porch, his eyes closed, his arms crossed over his chest.

I stomped up the steps.

He came awake on a start, jumping to his feet, then swaying with fatigue.

"You okay?" I asked him, grabbing for his arm to steady him.

He nodded. "Yeah, I'm just tired. Did the night guard last night."

Which meant the poor guy had been awake all night running the perimeter and had probably only got a few hours of sleep before he was needed for something else.

"I'll take over. You go home to bed."

"I've got night run on again tonight," he said.

I checked my cell phone for the time. "You can go home and get a few hours' sleep before then."

Markus sighed. "Thanks, Galen."

"Anytime," I said, patting him on the back.

I watched him walk away, then turned to stare through the door of the cabin.

Talia was sitting on the couch, cross legged, not doing anything. Just staring at me.

"Can I get you anything?" I called out to her.

"Yeah, a way out. Then my car keys."

I laughed. I couldn't help it. "Anything else?"

She pouted and I wanted to go up there and wipe that look right off her face. Preferably with a kiss.

I shook myself, growling in self-annoyance.

She's the asshole Maddox's mate. Pull yourself together.

"You okay?" she asked, standing up and walking toward the door opening.

I ran a frazzled hand through my hair. "Yeah. Just had a bad day. Do you need anything from the car? Clothes, perhaps?"

She inhaled deeply, her nostrils flaring as though she was controlling her temper. "Yes. I'd like my clothes."

Did I trust her not to make a break for it? No, I didn't.

"Tell me what you want and I'll get it for you."

She crossed her arms over her chest, which was more ample than I'd originally thought. I tried not to stare. "It would be easier if I just came out and grabbed the things I needed," she said.

I raised one eyebrow in her direction. "Can you guarantee me that once you get to your car, you'll just grab all your stuff and walk calmly and quietly back to the cabin?"

She lifted her chin, only a fraction of an inch, but part of me kind of loved the defiant streak. "Yes," she said.

I burst out laughing. "Sure you will. I'll just grab some shit and be back in a second."

I jogged back to my dad's place where we'd parked the car she'd been driving when I'd stopped her and grabbed a blanket and a suitcase. Then I trotted back to the front door of the cabin.

I didn't hesitate as I walked over the threshold and deposited her things at her feet. "Here you go."

Her pupils dilated as she stared at me, and I found myself wanting to grab hold of her. Which was insane. She wasn't mine to grab.

I backed away.

"Do you have witch in your blood?" I asked.

It wasn't unheard of for the witches to mix with the wolf shifters, though it was rare.

She frowned, before shaking her head and kneeling on the floor to open the huge suitcase I'd brought inside.

She started to take out clothes, choosing some new jeans to change into. "No. Both my parents were wolf shifters."

She glanced up at me as she got back to her feet holding a new top and some underwear.

I tried really hard not to stare at the bra she held. I was a grown man, after all. The sight of some basic, white, cotton underwear should not get my motor running like it suddenly was.

I took another step back.

Definitely a witch.

She tilted her head to the side and looked at me in an assessing way. "I wish I was a witch, then I'd be able to work out how to break that damn ward and get out of here."

I chuckled as I backed up over the threshold. "I think I'll stay here overnight. I'll sleep on the porch. Just in case your fiancé comes looking for you."

There was a flash of something that looked like hurt in her dark eyes, before she glanced down at her feet. I wasn't sure what it was, but it certainly looked like she was upset at the mention of her fated mate.

Maybe she was disappointed he hadn't started looking for her yet?

In fact, why hadn't he? If she was my mate, I'd have razed half the county to find her and get her back.

"Where's your cell phone?" I asked, realizing we hadn't checked her for one.

She picked up her jeans, clinging to the fresh clothes. "In the car, I think. I lost my old one and picked up a new one in town yesterday, but didn't have time to charge it or anything."

I frowned at her. Since when would someone travel as far as she had said she was going, without charging her phone? That made no sense at all.

"I'm going to go have a shower and get changed?" She phrased it as though it was a question.

I nodded, as if she were my guest. "Go for it. But the hot water will only last about three minutes. Fair warning."

That wasn't true, but I didn't want her disappearing for hours and using up my town's water supply.

"No problem," she said and bolted toward the bedroom.

I sat down on a chair on the porch, and the idea of a hidden cell phone began to play over and over in my head.

I got up off the chair and jogged down to her car. I checked the front seat, the back, and the trunk. No obvious sign of a new cell phone anywhere. Or an old one for that matter.

I looked back at the cabin. How could I have fallen for such an obvious trick? She could be on the phone to him right now telling him where she was, and how alone I was.

I ran back to the cabin, barged through the open front door, into the bedroom, and opened the closed bathroom door.

"What are you..." My accusation froze in my throat as her scream ricocheted around the bathroom walls.

She was completely naked beneath the spray of water, and she certainly wasn't holding a cell phone.

"*Get out!*"

I backed away, scanning the room for signs of a charger, or anything that would indicate she had a phone in here with her.

"I'm sorry," I managed to mumble. "I thought... never mind."

I bolted out of the room and slammed shut the door. Now *that* was an image that was seared onto my brain. How would I put that aside?

I huffed out a breath and began to look around the bedroom for anywhere she might have plugged in a phone: on the dresser, under the bed, and beneath the pillows. But there wasn't a cell, or device to be seen.

I grabbed my head with both hands and squeezed, trying to get the sight of Talia's gorgeous ass... perky breasts... perfect nipples... virgin body... out of my head.

"Damn it..."

I shook my head and bolted out of the cabin. Did I trust myself to sleep here with her within arm's reach all night?

I growled at myself. Of course, I did! I'd never taken a woman against her will in my life. Never would.

But damn, she was hot! Curved thighs. Tiny waist. Dark pink nipples.... I'd only gotten a flash of the front of her, before she turned her back and curled up against the tiles, showing me her perfectly rounded ass.

My God, she was beautiful.

Maddox was an idiot, for not turning up the second she went missing.

"Damn it all to hell."

She was an Alpha's mate, and I could see why. Just not *this* Alpha's mate. And that fact was going to drive me insane until I had her... or she escaped.

Whichever came first.

Chapter 12

Talia

I'd never been so mortified in my life, or embarrassed, than when the Alpha Galen walked in on me. Naked. No man had ever seen me like that. Not even Maddox.

I felt violated. But in the strangest way, I also felt safe.

The embarrassment in his eyes as his gaze raked my body had matched mine, I suspected.

Whatever he had rushed into the bathroom to do, it hadn't been to ravish me, either with my permission or against my will.

Galen's men so far had been respectful, but I'd been terrified to go to sleep. I'd imagined waking up to one of them in my bed, on top of me, hurting me in the most basic, horrible way.

But after seeing the way Galen had responded to finding me in the shower, I knew I was going to sleep okay tonight. He'd been so embarrassed his cheeks had flushed red and he'd bolted out of the bathroom so fast there had been a trail of smoke behind him.

Sure, he'd looked at me, *all of me*, but truth be told, I would have been hard pressed not to stare at him if I'd found him completely naked too.

I finished my shower, staying longer than three minutes just to test out what he'd said, despite the way my heart raced in my chest, and my shifter shimmered just beneath the surface, ready to jump into wolf form if the need arose.

When I crept into my room, I was wrapped in two towels, just to make sure Galen wouldn't see anything more than my ankles if he was sitting on my bed.

But he wasn't there. The room was eerily empty.

I dried myself and changed into a casual top and a pair of jeans from my suitcase, wishing I'd brought my slippers with me. And my dressing gown. But I hadn't exactly known what to pack for this trip, not to mention the fact that I'd been so out of it after Dad's death, my best friends had packed for me.

Once covered, I snuck out into the lounge to find it also empty. Disappointment hit me, hard. I was as shocked by the feeling as I was by the fact that he wasn't inside anymore.

Where did the disappointment stem from?

"Hello?" I called out.

Galen stuck his head in the front door, his eyes doing a cursory glance of my now dressed body, as if checking before he entered. Then he stepped into the room.

"My... apologies before," he began, tucking his hands behind his back. "I... I want you to know that despite the fact you're our prisoner, and your pack tried to kill me and my father and all of our male pack members, I would never harm you in... that way."

I liked the fact that he felt like he needed to say it. I couldn't really say why. Maybe because I understood what sort of life we led. That things got dangerous, and people got killed, and yet watching this huge man apologize for walking in on me naked was humbling.

He could have taken me if he'd wanted to. He still could. He was far stronger than me, and there was no one here to stop him.

I had the distinct impression he was pretty much the boss around here, even if there was an Alpha father somewhere in the background of the pack.

"I—"

He cut me off by lifting his hand and taking another step forward. "I swore to you yesterday that no one would hurt you, and I mean it. I..."

He shook his head, a frustrated growl coming from him.

It was a beautiful thing to see, watching his tough side war so fervently with his good side. He was an Alpha who would protect his women and children. I liked that in a man.

Unlike Maddox, a traitorous voice said in my head. *He didn't even try to protect his woman from the sentence of death.*

I bit the inside of my lip to punish myself for even thinking such nice things about my captor and such bad things about my ex-mate. What was wrong with me?

"All good. No harm done," I said. "Is there any food? I'm kinda starving."

He nodded, nipped out of the cabin, then a little while later, brought back into the room a huge plate covered with meat, bread, and potatoes.

My stomach growled at the smell of garlic and butter.

"Here you go."

I rushed toward him, taking the plate gratefully, though there wasn't a utensil to be seen. I didn't care.

"Thank you."

I hurried back to the couch and began making myself a lamb, or beef sandwich. I wasn't sure which one it was and I didn't care. It smelled delicious.

"I'll stay tonight," Galen said, although he'd already told me that.

I nodded and mumbled, "Okay."

He made it sound like he was protecting me, instead of what he was really doing, which was making sure I didn't escape.

The potatoes were warm and crisp, and even as I picked one up and bit into it, I moaned. Wow, that was awesome. Salty. Just how I liked them.

Galen didn't leave. Instead, he wandered to the end of the couch and sat down, and watched me eat. Strangely, I didn't get self-conscious. I figured he had to deal with the sight of my hunger since he was the reason I was so starving.

I ate all the meat, half the potatoes, and most of the bread too.

"Is this bread homemade?" I asked, staring down at a crust dripping with butter. It didn't look like something bought from a shop.

"Yes," he said, smiling softly. "My dad's next-door neighbor is a great cook. She brings food over all the time."

I chewed on the end of the bread. "Where's your mom?"

I was pretty sure I knew the answer, but part of me wanted the personal conversation. Wanted the connection in this lonely, devastating time.

I shouldn't feel that way about Galen, of course. He was the enemy. But since Maddox had thrown me out so spectacularly, I found myself yearning for any type of contact. Even with a kidnapper.

Galen sighed. "She died about ten years ago."

I bit my lip and mimicked his sigh, leaning back against the couch. "Mine too. And now that Dad's gone, I suppose I'm an orphan."

Galen didn't respond, so I took the platter to the sink and did a quick wash. Then I lay it on the couch cushion next to him. When he didn't move, I sat back down in my original spot.

The room was still warm, despite the fact it was dark outside now.

"Where's your dad?" I asked, wondering where the true Alpha was in all of this.

Most wolf packs, like the one I'd grown up in, only had one leader. And he stayed the Alpha until the day he died, or someone came in and took the title from him.

Maddox had said something about Galen's dad being sick. Maybe? I couldn't really remember now. The last week had turned into an absolute blur of a mess in my head. I still couldn't remember why my pack had attacked Galen's in the first place, let alone everything that had followed.

"He's, um..." Galen faltered, sliding a hand over his neck and tugging at his hair as though frustrated.

"Is he okay?" I asked, pulling my legs up and wrapping my arms around them.

I was feeling sleepy now. My belly was full, and after the rush of adrenaline from the shower mishap, I was coming down and wanting to rest.

I laid my head on the tops of my knees and stared at the big shifter, who was so much more attractive that I'd first thought. He had hair that curled down to his jaw line. And his eyes were so intense.

When he finally turned to look at me, his jaw was tight, his teeth clenched. He looked angry, but I could already tell it wasn't at me.

"My dad's... sick. He got taken to hospital this morning. That's why I've been gone all day. I was with him."

I sat up, slipping my legs down. "Oh, I'm so sorry. That must be... strange. I mean, for an Alpha to get sick. It's unusual. Isn't it?"

Galen nodded, swallowing so hard his Adam's apple bobbed up and down.

"Yeah, it is. And no one can work out what's wrong with him. It's just..." He tapped his heels on the ground a few times. "It's not good."

Then his gaze slid to me, and this time I could see the anger banked inside his dark eyes. "I believe that's why your pack attacked us. They think, with my dad sick, that we're weak. That we don't have an Alpha at the helm any longer, but they're wrong. We do."

He stood up, and sudden fear quickened my blood stream.

His hands were clenched, and the set of his jaw told me how upset he was about everything that had happened.

"I'm sorry," I said, though I wasn't sure how I could have changed either scenario.

Galen walked toward the door, then doubled back and paced along the wall, behind the couch. "I know it's not your fault. It's obvious your pack keeps you in the dark about these things. But you need to know, we're not weak! We killed at least ten of your men, and you only got two of ours, and *we* weren't expecting it."

Pain and tears clogged my throat. "I'm sorry for your loss. I promise, I didn't know anything about the attack. And I lost my father that day too."

Galen stopped pacing. "My pack killed your father?"

"No. He made it back to the pack..." How did I say this without outright lying? "But he died shortly after. I know it's not your fault. So please don't blame me for what happened either."

I wrapped my arms around myself and squeezed tight. "I lost so much that day, and because I'm just a girl, they didn't tell me anything! I couldn't prepare myself... I didn't know..."

The sobs began to rise in my throat and I couldn't stop them this time.

Galen strode across the room, yanked me to my feet, and held me in his arms.

I pressed myself into him, crying against his huge chest. And this time I didn't fight the grief, nor stop myself from mourning my father the way I needed to. They'd taken him from me. I wasn't ready. It hadn't been his time.

It wasn't fair.

I'd lost everything, and I'd done nothing wrong. I'd loved my father. I'd loved Maddox. I'd been kind, and loyal, the best person I knew how to be, and everything I'd been taught made up a good female pack member.

And this was how they repaid me? Killing my only remaining parent, and taking away my future, and my past, in one fell swoop.

Galen held my head to his chest and murmured, "Shh..." as I cried until I was exhausted and could barely stand from the pain in my heart.

He picked me up and carried me to the bed. I lay limp in his arms, too devastated to consider what I was doing. He lay me down and pulled up the blankets like I was child and he was caring for me.

I felt numb. Dead inside. I could barely see through my aching, tear-filled eyes.

"I'll go sleep on the couch," Galen murmured as he backed toward the door. "But if they need me at the hospital, I'll have to leave."

I nodded and turned onto my side, nestling into the pillows.

I wasn't sure why he was being so nice to me, but I wasn't looking a gift horse in the mouth after all the bad luck I'd had lately.

"Thank you," I managed to choke out. "You've been very kind, Galen."

I would figure all this out in the morning and decide what to do. For now, I closed my eyes and fell asleep, dreaming of big black wolves… and death.

Chapter 13

Galen

When I woke up around sunrise, my neck ached, and I couldn't feel my left arm.

I rolled off the uncomfortable couch and landed as quietly as I could so I didn't wake the girl sleeping in the room next door.

"Ouch." I stretched out my neck and hung my arm down straight to let the nerve flow connect back to my brain.

The I shook the dead arm because I hated how it felt.

Feeling came back in electrical pulsing bursts. I got to my feet and groaned. Last night was not the best night's sleep I'd ever had, but strangely, it wasn't the worst either.

"You've been so kind, Galen." Her voice kept replaying, over and over in my head. She had sounded so forlorn; so broken.

Where was that fucking mate of hers? Why hadn't he come to rescue her?

Comforting Talia had been weirdly soothing to me. I was surrounded by stress and pain with my dad and everything else that was happening at the moment, and feeling helpless about so many things.

But with her last night, I'd been able to help her, comfort her, and that had made the big wolf inside me happy.

Which confused me even more. She wasn't my woman; she wasn't even of my pack. It shouldn't have felt so good to be with her.

I walked to the bedroom door, which was still wide open, and stared into the room. Talia was lying on the bed, the blankets flung back and her face resting in sleep. Her lips were slightly open and her gorgeous red hair was spread across the pillows.

I turned away before I could admit that what I was feeling was close to passion, or lust, or desire.

I refused to covet another man's wife. Even if they weren't yet married. It just wasn't acceptable. I wasn't religious by any stretch, but the original commandments were a pretty solid way to live your life, in my view.

There was a knock on the front door, then David stepped into the room.

I pulled shut the bedroom door. "Hey man. You here to take over?"

David nodded. "Yeah, if you want me to."

"Please do. I need to go into town, check on my dad and the bar." I needed to work tonight. There were only so many nights I could let the bar staff run things without me.

"Cool. Anything you want me to do? Specifically?"

"Yeah, make sure she's fed. And don't touch her."

David's eyebrows shot up. "Touch her? Why would I touch her?"

I huffed out a laugh. David was into guys; always had been. "Sorry, man, I just mean... you know. Leave her alone."

"Easy," he said, and walked back into the sunshine. "I'll just sit on the porch until you get back."

Concern coursed through me which I tried to squash. No point worrying over a woman who was our prisoner. She couldn't escape. And with David outside, no one would get in.

"I might send one of the witches here to check on the wards, just to make sure they'll hold up against an attack if Talia's pack come to get her."

"Talia?"

Oh, crap.

I tried for a casual shrug. "Yeah. That's her name. I won't be long man, thanks."

I waved goodbye and jogged down the steps.

I needed to be rid of the strange level of protectiveness I felt around Talia. She was the enemy, but my wolf didn't seem to care. I liked her. She seemed... sweet. And bright. And loyal to a fault.

Great qualities in a mate.

"Oh, shut up." I growled at myself. "She's already somebody else's!"

And the last time I'd had the chance at a great mate, I'd failed to protect her.

I didn't deserve another.

In my truck, I sped off toward town, not bothering to look at the speed limit. I could tell by the way the trees were flying by that I wasn't doing anywhere near as low as sixty.

I went into the hospital, where I was advised that Dad's condition hadn't changed. He was still on oxygen, and although the nurses said he'd woken up once or twice, he was sound asleep now, and I wasn't going to wake him again.

I checked on the bar, and everything was as it was when I left it a few days ago. I made a few phone calls and got my manager and best barman in for the night. I'd open, but I wouldn't necessarily be there for the whole time.

I'd trained some good staff, mostly humans from town, and some shifters from my pack. The bar ran like a well-oiled machine, with or without me at the helm.

I had just gotten the bar in order, when someone knocked on the locked front door. I yanked open the door and startled.

"Maybelle," I said, greeting the witch who had always been a friend of our pack. "I was thinking of calling you this morning."

I held open the door, and she drifted in. "I know. I could sense your need for me." She glanced around the room, narrowing her eyes as though looking for a problem. "How can I help you?"

I grinned at the powerful mage. We paid her well, in money, liquor, whatever she wanted. And she had helped us out with her magic skills a number of times over the years.

"I have a prisoner, from a neighboring pack, that I'm keeping in the cabin. I wanted to make sure the wards you set up last year are still holding strong."

Maybelle sniffed the air, then slid toward me. "You smell... different."

I crossed my arms over my chest. "Yeah, sorry. I'll have a shower as soon as I can."

"No, it's not that. I can smell another shifter on you, and she's.... odd."

I frowned at the witch. "What do you mean?"

Maybelle took another sniff. "I mean, she's not a normal shifter."

"I don't understand." I frowned. As far as I could tell, Talia was perfect.

Maybelle stepped away, her eyes swirling with the purple of her magic. "I don't understand, either. I would like to meet her."

"Yes. Please. I need you to check the cabin also. I want to know that if her pack tries to rescue her, they won't be able to pass the threshold."

Maybelle nodded. "I can do that, but perhaps, tomorrow?"

I didn't question her. She was an odd creature, and did things at her own pace. If she didn't think there was any urgency to the situation with Talia, I trusted her judgment.

"Thank you, Maybelle."

She stepped toward the door, then glanced back at me. "Has your father told you of the demons that roam in our world?"

I froze and stared at her, the hairs on the back of my neck standing on end. Was this one of her weird premonition things? Another spanner in the works was the last thing we needed right now. "Ah... yes. He has. Though I've never seen one."

Demons were evil. Everyone agreed on that, at least. They were part of the paranormal world, of course, but unlike the rest of us, demons worshipped only darkness.

Maybelle stared into my eyes. "You will. I've sensed them moving around, testing people."

"What should I do when I see one?" I asked her, not having any idea what the answer would be. Were they deadly to *us*? Should I be concerned for my pack? Could I even kill one if I wanted to?

"Do not be afraid of it," she said. "They are here only as scouts; messengers for their evil masters. They won't hurt one such as you."

Then she swept out of the room without another backwards glance. I sighed. Witches were strange, and I could never quite work out how their minds worked. Though they often came in handy when it came to magic needs relating to the pack. I filed away all the information Maybelle had just given me, and got back to what I was meant to be doing.

Sorting out the bar.

After more phone calls, I ran up the stairs behind the bar that led to my small apartment on the top floor and had a quick shower. I scrubbed my skin, wondering what Maybelle had meant about Talia smelling strange.

Was it possible that Maybelle had sensed the girl wasn't mine? Or from my pack's blood lines? Or was it something else? I didn't try to guess further, and pushed the questions to the back of my mind.

Too many other things to question, and the way of the witches wasn't mine to question.

I put on a fresh change of clothes, packed up some boxes of whiskey and bourbon, and got in the car. I was strangely excited to be going back to the pack, though it annoyed me that part of the reason was because I wanted to see Talia so much.

It was wrong.

She was taken. Mated. And not to me. When I arrived home, a guy was sitting on the steps of my father's house. I'd never seen him before. He wore a black leather jacket and had a buzz cut, which made his dark eyes stand out even more.

I smelt the shifter on him, but like Talia, he wasn't one of mine.

A lone wolf. A shifter and—I had the feeling—a dangerous being.

I parked the truck and got out. "Hey."

No one usually visited our pack unless they were family members. And if they were family, they wouldn't be sitting on the Alpha's front step, waiting for who knows what.

The guy got to his feet. He was a good six feet tall and built well, like many of my betas.

He didn't seem to be an Alpha, but he wasn't necessarily a follower, either.

"Can I help you?" I asked, walking right up to him and looking down from my six-foot-six height in obvious challenge.

He grinned up at me, as if aware of my ploy and not fazed. "I'm Darius. I came to speak to the Alpha about joining your pack."

"Well, my father's not here at the moment, so you've got me in his stead." I narrowed my eyes at him. "Any reason you want to join our pack?"

Darius nodded. "I've been traveling across the state, but I'm sick and tired of the constant moving. Always looking out, with no one to watch my back. I need to set down some roots. And I heard good things about your pack."

My brows rose. I didn't necessarily believe or disbelieve him. It could be the truth. But a grain of skepticism was always healthy. "And the reason you can't go home?" I drilled.

His smile faltered. "Well, I... My mate died last year. In childbirth. I... can't go back. Too many bad memories."

His words sliced across my heart with the keen sharpness of a knife.

I dropped my arms down and cleared my throat with a rough cough. "Sorry to hear about that."

He shrugged. "Thanks."

I glanced around, still suspicious about his timing. "Any reason you chose our pack over the other three in the area?"

Darius didn't seem to miss a beat. "I did speak to one other pack before coming here, but they're in a bit of a messy state, and I don't want to join anyone else's drama. Plus, I'd rather be on the winning side."

I raised an eyebrow. "Because you need protecting?"

Darius laughed. "Nah. I do like a good fight."

He looked like he could handle himself too. Despite the baggy leather jacket, I could see the strength in his legs and in his core. This guy knew his way around a gym, or he'd done some serious outdoor work, over a long period of time.

"Okay. I'll give you a week to prove you're not going to be a nuisance, and you can bunk in with some of the other bachelors in town. My Beta Markus has a spare room at his place."

Darius grinned. "I appreciate the opportunity."

"Is there any other reason you chose our pack?" I asked, still worried about this stranger's reason for coming here right now.

"Well, two actually. I heard you run a bar in town, and I know my way around a drink pourer. And a hot grill."

That was good to know. "And the second reason?"

"Well, I had some news I wanted to share with you, though I didn't want to just come out with it at the start. You'd think I was some sort of snitch."

I crossed my arms over my chest and narrowed my eyes. I wanted to convey my thoughts about snitches, though at the same time I wasn't going to ignore Darius if he knew something I needed to know too. The pack came before my pride.

"I've already said you can stay, so if you wanna tell me something extra, now's the time."

He shrugged off his jacket and pulled out a packet of cigarettes. "You mind?"

I shook my head. "It's your life."

He huffed out a laugh, then lit his cigarette. "You're right."

He inhaled deeply, then blew out the smoke in the opposite direction to where I was standing.

He was definitely fit and strong, but it would take me at least a week to determine his character. For all I knew, he was a pack member of our nearby enemies. I didn't know all of them by sight.

Though, I was pretty sure I'd have recognized him if I'd ever seen him in town, or in my bar, before now. And I hadn't.

"So?" I prompted.

He stared at me. "The other pack I tried to join, they're in a mess, right?"

"Yeah," I said, assuming he meant our lovely neighbors. Talia's pack. "They attacked us, and we fought back. They lost a lot of men."

He nodded. "Yeah, but it's not just that."

"What, then?"

"They're hunting someone."

Hunting someone? Didn't he mean, hunting for someone? I narrowed my eyes. "Who?"

I assumed it must be Talia. I mean, why wouldn't they be hunting for her? I was astounded they hadn't come for her yet. Not that she would have been easy to follow, the way she'd been driving.

"The Alpha's son's former fated mate. They threw her out of the pack, and gave her three days to leave town. But they can feel her, and they know she's still around. They have orders to kill her on sight."

Former fated mate? Maddox had *rejected* her? My mouth dropped open. It must have been the other way round. Surely, it must have been Talia who rejected that loser, Maddox. "They're looking for Talia... to kill her?"

How was that possible? What on earth could that girl have done to receive that sort of wrath?

"You know who they're looking for?"

I nodded. "Yeah." I rubbed the space between my brows, trying to will away a sudden headache. "I grabbed her the other night. One of my Betas knew who she was, but she seemed to be headed out of the state and I thought... *Fuck*."

I'd stopped her from leaving town. She'd been running away from her pack. If they'd given her three days to get away...

She'd hit the deadline and it'd passed her by some time ago.

I grabbed my head on both sides of my skull and squeezed hard. "Shit."

What the hell was she playing at? Pretending she was still important to her pack? Though she had offered to leave, and not look back, hadn't she? Had that been the truth? Was she really heading to an aunt in Wichita?

What had she lied about?

"Thanks for letting me know, man. I'll introduce you to some of the guys, then I better go deal with Talia."

I found Darius somewhere to sleep, and introduced him around. Then I headed back to the cabin, fire in my belly and anger clenching my fists. What the hell was this shit?

She must've been lying from the moment I got her. So, what was the truth? And could I trust her to tell me anyway?

I stormed up the steps and into the cabin.

Talia was lying on her belly on the rug, reading a book. Her feet were crossed, and her gorgeous thick hair was out and flowing down her back.

My heart hurt just to look at her.

She looked up at me, startled.

"You need to tell me what's going on," I said, putting a growl into the words.

She jumped to her feet, her eyes huge and suddenly fearful.

"What do you mean?" she whispered.

"I just found out that your pack is hunting you and you're to be killed on sight. And... ex fated mate? What the fuck is that about, Talia? I thought you were set to marry the next Alpha of your pack."

She chewed on her bottom lip, a tremble going through her body. I could practically smell the fear on her.

"I was."

"What? Speak up."

"I was!" she said, more forcefully, before wrapping her arms around her middle.

"Well, what the hell happened?"

This was a fucking mess. Here I was trying to avenge my pack and fulfil a promise to my father without killing more people, and the plan had gone up in smoke.

Worse than that. I'd stopped her from escaping their clutches, and most likely signed her death warrant, so I'd truly screwed up on that front, too.

"I... He..."

"Spit it out!"

She jumped. "I...I..."

She stopped, swallowing, and I couldn't take any more.

"Argh! I'm going for a run," I said, unable to get a hold of my temper. It was all too much. Too many mistakes. Some of them fair and square in my court.

I ripped off my shirt, noting the way her pupils dilated when she saw me half naked. Another thing to be pissed about. All this time, she was available, and I hadn't even known it. Fated mate be damned.

She was a *rejected* mate.

And now she was in danger. This was a lethal combination for the protector in me.

"I'll be back later."

I ran out the door and leapt off the patio, shifting halfway through the air, and landed with my paws on the dirt.

I took off.

What a fucking mess this was.

Chapter 14

Talia

Oh, my God. He looked so furious. *He's going to kill me when he gets back.*

The only thing that had been keeping me alive was the fact that I was Maddox's mate, and therefore useful to Galen.

And now, he had somehow found out the truth.

I paced up and down the room, my book and my relaxed mood now totally forgotten. I wasn't safe anymore and thanks to the witch's wards, I was still trapped.

My wolf rose up within me, and for the first time, I didn't try and stop my shifter from bursting through. My jeans and tank top shredded as my black wolf emerged.

My heart was pounding so fast I was shaking.

"What the..." One of Galen's Betas stepped over the threshold, and I saw my opportunity to escape.

I hadn't been able to get past the threshold last time, but with one of their pack short circuiting the magic, and with me in wolf form, I had a chance.

I ran for the door. The guy tried to stop me, putting his arms out, holding tight to the door frame.

Perfect. Thank you.

I leapt through the air, pushing my two front paws into the guy's chest, and both of us sailed through the door and onto the ground.

I shook myself, looking around the area for a way out.

I'd made it out of the cabin, but I had to go. I had to leave everything behind. My life was at stake now. Not just from my pack, but from Galen's as well.

Two wolf shifter packs would be after me.

What chance did I have, to survive even a few hours, let alone through the night?

I turned toward town and started running. My old pack would get me if I went anywhere near the forest. But the town provided a neutral zone for all the packs. My only chance at this point was to reach neutral ground. Maybe Kylie would hide me again, until things died down a little?

At this point I didn't know. And I didn't care.

All I knew was, I had to get away from Galen and his pack, right now.

I ran down the road, dodging people and traffic, my heart pounding like a steam engine.

I ended up at a fork in the road that I didn't recognize. Both road signs said they led to town, but which way would keep me safe from Maddox's pack?

A commotion came from behind me, from the direction of the cabin I'd been staying in. I could hear fighting and yelling. Then the howl of a wolf sounded, long and mournful.

The sound called to my essence; my blood. I almost turned and ran back to greet the caller, having to use all my willpower to stop.

Fuck.

I shivered. Galen knew I was gone. I had to keep running, and not into town. I needed to put distance between me and the Alpha's son.

Both of the Alpha heirs.

I ran through the forest and away from the town, in the opposite direction of Galen's pack.

Oh, shit.

They caught up to me before I had gone anywhere near far enough. I didn't know whose land I was on—Galen's, Maddox's, or the neutral zone—but it didn't matter. I was surrounded.

I was going to die.

Three white wolves came at me from all sides. I panted, backing up. From their scent, I could tell without even looking at their familiar wolf forms that two of them were Maddox's Betas, young guys I'd known my whole life. How did they justify chasing me, let alone getting ready to kill me? We had been friends, in the past. I couldn't fathom trying to kill a friend.

I whined, to show them I was scared. That I was defenseless. We'd never been taught to fight in my pack. The women didn't do that.

Instead of showing any care or compassion, they snarled back at me, and I yelped. Panic set in. They were serious. They were really going to follow the Alpha's decree.

Where could I go?

The largest wolf showed me his teeth. I turned tail and ran. They caught me easily and knocked me down into the dirt.

I growled and turned, but one of them grabbed my back leg, biting into the flesh and hauling me along the ground. I cried out at the pain, kicking my other leg in an attempt to be free.

A third wolf stalked over to me. He was older and huge. One of the Alpha's council members, by the looks of him.

I stared up at him and whined. He growled, his lip quivering as he showed me his white sharp teeth.

There would be no mercy. I was going to die today, at the hands—or teeth and claws—of my own pack. And I had no one to blame except myself. They had given me time to escape, and I'd squandered much of it, before being stupid enough to be captured by Galen and his men.

A loud, threatening growl rolled over me like thunder in the distance. The white wolves looked up.

The large Beta was hit in the chest by a huge black wolf, and rolled backwards, knocked off his feet.

The possible reprieve gave me added strength, and I fought with the wolf holding my leg, snapping my jaws at him until he let go. I jumped to my feet and growled, watching in awe as the black wolf took on all three of the smaller white wolves at once.

He headbutted them and snapped his jaws, biting at their necks with his razor-sharp teeth.

The two smaller wolves were bleeding and limping, but the larger one recovered more quickly, and stalked toward the black wolf that I had to assume was Galen.

He was magnificent—and terrifying.

Galen charged and grabbed the largest Beta around the throat, lifting him high. He shook him like a rag doll and dropped him. With a snarl, he tore the Beta's throat out with a vicious tug and snap of his neck.

It was over, just like that.

He threw back his head and howled, his jaws soaked with blood, and I gaped at the scene before me.

Blood and guts everywhere, and the triumphant black wolf in the middle of it all, breathing hard.

The large Beta was obviously dead, his chest no longer rising and falling. Only then did Galen shift back.

I couldn't help but stare at him.

He was dripping with sweat, naked, and shaking with adrenaline. He was a warrior standing over the fallen body of his enemy on a battlefield.

I let go of my wolf even though all my instincts told me not to, and shifted back to human. Naked, and vulnerable, and crouched on the ground at Galen's feet, but no longer afraid. Not when Galen had just charged in to save me.

I stared at him, wanting to say thanks but unable to formulate words. No one had ever stood up for me, the way he had just done. Not even Maddox. *Especially* not Maddox.

He was panting, and blood dripped from wounds in his flank and his side.

When he turned to face me properly, his eyes were still shifted. "I fucking hate killing those bastards."

He spat on the ground, more blood painting the earth.

I was shaking as well as naked, but Galen didn't have desire in his eyes as he stared at me.

"Thank you, for saving me," I said through my chattering teeth, finally managing to get the words out.

What else could I say? He really had saved my life. I owed him, big time.

I swallowed hard and forced myself to calm down. *Talk rationally. We're naked, surrounded by blood and guts, but we need to remain calm.*

"How can I repay you?" I asked as I sat up slowly. "I can go, if you want me to. Now. If you'll let me grab my dad's car, I can leave right away. Go to my aunt in Wichita like I'd planned."

Galen shook his head and bent down toward me, fierce and strong. "No, you'll never make it. Your old pack will hunt you down well before you hit state lines."

"I have to try." I began to sob, biting my lip. "I don't have anywhere else to go. My mom's gone... my dad too. There's no one else. The only family I have left is in Wichita. Galen, please. Let me go. I have nothing... and no one..." My voice cracked, and I stopped. I couldn't be any more pathetic, begging at his feet like this.

Quickly I got to my feet.

He ran a hand through his hair, pushing the thick curls off his forehead. "I'm offering you a place in my pack, Talia. Come back with me. I'll protect you."

Shock pulsed through me. "You'd really do that?"

Tears of gratitude burned in my eyes. How was it possible that after the ugly twist of human nature I'd seen in my own pack over the past few days, Galen—the enemy—could be so different?

He nodded. "I would do that, and I am. Come home with me. Be a part of my pack."

I wrapped my arms around my shivering body. "But... why?"

He shrugged, his eyes finally shifting back to completely human. "Because you need us. And I like you. I think you would fit in well with us. Do I have to give you another reason? Do you really want to travel all the way to Wichita, and live outside a pack, in a mostly human environment?"

I shook my head and held in the sob that rose. He liked me? I liked him too. He was a good man—he had shown that in many ways even in the short time I'd known him—and he would be a fantastic Alpha when the time came to inherit the throne from his father.

"I... accept. Thank you."

My heart, which had been so broken a few days ago, filled up to the point that I could barely speak.

He nodded once. "Let's shift, and get back to the pack. It's safer that way, assuming you can travel in wolf form?"

I nodded. "Of course I can. And I'd be honored to run beside you."

He grinned, then chuckled. "I feel a strange amount of protectiveness over you. And I'd prefer if the rest of the pack didn't see you like this."

He indicated my nakedness and I laughed, an unfamiliar weightlessness filling my chest. I couldn't remember the last time I had felt so cared for.

I should never have survived these few days, not with so many things against me. My dad's mistakes. My pack's blood lust. Galen's need for revenge.

Somehow, I'd made it through everything. So far.

I had the feeling I was still on borrowed time, though.

I smiled at the man who had officially just become my hero. "I have to tell you something, Galen. Even if I feel that it is inappropriate to say, I believe I owe you the truth."

"Tell me."

His jaw became tight, as if I was about to deliver news that was hard to take, or bad.

I laughed to try and break some of the tension. "You're the only man who has ever seen me naked. So yeah, I'd appreciate it if you don't show me off to the rest of the pack like this."

I held my arms out and shrugged, with the intention to show off my lackluster breasts and wobbling stomach.

Galen's gaze, now that it was human, flared suddenly. There was more lust in his eyes than I was comfortable with. But I stood, proudly, a new member of his pack.

Galen dragged his fingers down his face. "For fuck's sake, Talia. Don't say things like that."

I didn't respond. I just let go of my human body and dropped down into my wolf.

Then Galen transformed before me.

His huge black wolf stood beside me, towering above in a much larger form than mine, then he threw back his head and howled.

I shivered.

All that power. He was incredible.

I looked once at the dead white wolf lying on the ground, then shook my head and turned away.

I followed Galen back to his pack, my new home.

Chapter 15

Galen

I took Talia back to the cabin to gather her clothes from her suitcase, and to my father's house to gather mine. Being naked in front of that girl was far too dangerous. She was too beautiful, and now that I knew she was available, my wolf howled for her.

And that comment about being the only man who'd ever seen her naked? For fuck's sake, the girl would drive me insane with comments like that! My wolf practically leapt with joy inside my chest.

I commanded my Betas to meet me at the bar, got Talia to drive her car behind me, and we all met at my place. I figured we could both stay there for a while. I would be close to the hospital, and with the weekend coming, I had to work.

"So, you said you work here?" Talia asked, glancing up at the sign outside my bar that read, 'Howling Wolf'.

"Yeah... kind of," I said, unlocking the front door so that everyone else could join us for a meeting. "I own the bar, and the apartment above it. I live up there."

She stared at me, surprise in her wide eyes.

Before I could answer the unspoken questions in the air, the front door opened, and Markus, David, and the new recruit Darius, wandered in.

"Hey guys. Come grab a seat. I want you to officially meet Talia, and work out our next move."

The three Betas came over to where we hung out around the bar and grabbed bar stools.

"Hey," David said, lifting his chin in greeting to Talia.

She jumped up and sat on the bar top, her legs dangling like a kid sitting on a ledge.

"Hi."

I shook my head. She seemed to effortlessly manage a fantastic combination of naivety and sensual allure.

I turned away from her so that I could focus on what I needed to say. "Guys, this is Talia. I've offered her sanctuary within our pack."

"Sanctuary?" Markus repeated. "Why does she need—"

"Talia is going to stay here, with me," I said, interrupting Markus. I didn't need to explain myself to him. Then I heard my words as though from another place.

I tightened my jaw. I hadn't expected to say it just like that, but now that I had, I wasn't taking it back. "She needs our help and we're going to give it. Her pack is after her. They plan to kill her if they catch her, and since we now share a common enemy, that makes us allies."

The guys, to their credit, took my news in their stride. Mostly. The only show of surprise was a couple of raised eyebrows, and surreptitious glances at Talia.

"So, what do you need from us?" David asked.

"Help," I said simply. "I want Talia kept safe. She knows her pack well, and will be key in our revenge, and in staying one step ahead of them."

I glanced up at Talia, who nodded once. We hadn't actually discussed her helping me get revenge on them for attacking our pack, but she seemed solid in relation to the idea, and I appreciated her not contradicting me in front of my Betas.

The guys and I talked about how we were going to obtain the revenge we sought, and threw around a whole lot of suggestions. We went back and forth, and in the end, came up with a few ideas, but no actual solution. Not yet.

Talia got up about halfway through the discussion and wandered around the bar, trailing her fingers over the furniture. Concern was etched on her face. I wondered if she was concerned about her old pack, or something else.

I would ask her, as soon as we finished here.

"Galen, I'm going for a quick walk," she whispered, once she had circled back to me. Then she spoke more loudly, for everyone to hear. "Do you guys want anything from the bakery?"

I shook my head, as did the others. "No," I confirmed. "Do you need any money or anything?"

"No. I've got my own. I won't be long." She smiled at the guys, then slipped out the front door.

The bakery was nearby, and this was neutral ground, in town. She'd be safe enough for now.

As soon as the door closed, Markus turned to me. "What's with you and her?"

I took a sip of my beer, then shrugged. "Nothing. What do you mean?"

Markus and David glanced at each other. "You're acting kinda... possessive toward her. I mean, she's cute and all, but she's the other Alpha's mate."

I clamped my jaw down. "Not anymore."

I leaned back in my chair and crossed my arms over my chest. They needed to shut up about her being another Alpha's mate. It was in the past.

Markus's jaw dropped. "What do you mean?"

I groaned, not sure I should be the one to tell them Talia's news, but what choice did I have? They'd find out soon enough.

"The Alpha of their pack rejected her. They've kicked her out."

"What?" Markus said, then grunted. "Those bastards."

"It's true," Darius said, finally speaking up. "I heard it straight from some of their Betas when I met them the other day. It was a love match. Fated mates. So, she must be pretty devastated, if her mate has rejected her."

There was silence around us as everyone in the room digested the new information. I hadn't really thought about what Talia must feel about her breakup.

"We better head back," Markus said, jumping to his feet.

"Darius," I said, "you interested in working a shift tonight in the bar? If I'm going to watch Talia, then I need an extra hand here."

I'd still need to work, but an extra set of eyes on the drinks, and the guys starting brawls, was always handy. Especially if I was running upstairs regularly to check on my new pack member.

"Yeah. Of course," he said. "Can you show me where things are now?"

I nodded. "Sure."

Markus and David headed home, and Darius came around behind the bar and started going through the stock with me.

Then it occurred to me that Talia wasn't back yet.

"Hey, how long's Talia been gone?" I asked, walking back around to the front of the bar.

"Don't know." Darius tucked a cigarette behind his ear. "Do you think she might be in trouble?"

"No, the wolf packs around here have laws about fights in town. It's a neutral zone," I explained. "There'd be hell to pay if they broke that law. We all have to abide by it."

Darius shrugged. "Yeah, but she's a single female, on her own. And her whole pack is out to get her. Can you guarantee they'll all toe the line?"

My gut clenched tight, and my heart sunk.

No. I couldn't guarantee anything, when it came to another wolf pack.

Why had I let her stroll out the door like that? If anything had happened to her, it would be on me.

My wolf surged to the surface and I forced it back down. Here in town, I needed to stay human.

"I've gotta go." I raced for the door and pulled it open. "Where the hell did she say she was going?"

Darius came up behind me, even though I hadn't asked him to back me up. "The bakery, or something like that."

"Yes, that's right." I raced off.

The bakery was on the next block. With Darius hot on my heels, I ran down the street in search of our lost wolf.

TALIA

I didn't know how to repay Galen and his pack for their kindness. Until I remembered how much the male shifters in my old pack liked their food. These guys would surely be the same. A trip to the bakery was the least I could do to say thanks.

I didn't just go to the bakery. Considering Galen had saved my life, I thought he deserved a bit more food in his belly than a few pies. And his pack members as well.

I didn't have a kitchen, but I could get them some treats. I had money, thanks to Dad. So I went to the bakery, the fruit and vegetable market, and then the candy shop.

My arms loaded with food, I began the trek back to Galen's bar.

I headed down an alleyway that would save me time in my trip back. I knew this town; it was neutral, and therefore safe.

Dark silhouettes in the distance emerged from the shadows and out walked three large men I recognized. All in their thirties. All from my old pack. Noah had a shaved head and an orange-tinged beard. Justin was blond and quiet; while Reed had dark eyes and dark hair.

They were all deadly.

I froze.

Their faces lit up when they saw me, like it was the fourth of July.

They shared a look and the way they licked their lips in preparation of the kill made my stomach lurch and my heart begin to pound. I dropped the bags I was carrying.

There were too many of them to take on alone, and yet I didn't want to simply run away. They would only chase me down, and getting them excited by the hunt wasn't a good idea.

I could do this. I just had to stay calm. *Breathe.* Maybe I could talk my way out of this. After all, we were in town.

I picked up the bags and with careful, deliberate steps, began to back out of the alley.

"Hey! Traitor! Where are you going?" Reed called out.

I kept walking, faster. My heart pounded in my chest, but I didn't dare shift. We had rules, after all.

Running footsteps thudded behind me. A large hand grabbed my shoulder and pulled me back.

The food went flying, the paper bags breaking open and pastries spilling over the cobblestone path.

I spun to face them, my hands tightening into fists. They hadn't shifted yet, and I assumed that was because of the rules about town. None of the humans were allowed to see us in wolf form.

But I was one girl up against three guys. It didn't matter whether we were in wolf or human form. They outnumbered me, and would outperform in strength, ten times over.

Galen, where are you?

"What's up?" I managed , though my stomach was tight and fear made my pulse quicken.

"What's up?" Noah asked, sauntering closer. "Why are you still here? You're meant to be long gone. You were given fair warning."

Reed was on my right, and he advanced on me. I took a step back, feeling a stone wall at my spine.

Damn, I was trapped.

"I was meant to be over the border by now," I whispered, trying to keep them talking while I worked out a plan. "But I had car troubles and had to come back to sort it out."

'Car troubles' was one way of explaining what had happened, I supposed.

"You should have gone while you had the chance," Noah said. "Now we're gonna have to kill you, because the Alpha wishes it."

I swallowed hard, standing as tall as I could, even as they pressed in from all sides. My hands clutched at the wall, seeking to draw on its strength. "But the town is a neutral zone," I said. "Like Switzerland."

Or that was how it had always been explained to us.

Justin took a couple of steps back. "She's right, guys."

"Yeah, but who's gonna know?" Reed said, his nasty face twisting up into a scowl. "The Alpha wants her dead, and his word is law."

"But—" I began.

Noah whacked me across the face.

I staggered sideways, my eye exploding with pain.

I stumbled away, trying to keep my balance and stay on my feet, but also trying to break up the little pack hunt they had going on.

"You need to stop," I said, squinting at them with my bad eye. "You aren't allowed to attack me here in town."

Justin hung back, a worried frown on his face, but Noah and Reed advanced on me. Their sneers were matching. "The rules are there to protect our packs. But if no one shifts, you're just a girl who got mugged in an alleyway," Noah said.

Reed swung his fist at me. I only just managed to duck out of the way.

They were serious. They were going to beat me to death right here and now, and blame it on a robbery gone wrong.

"What? So, you're just gonna leave my dead body in the alley?" I asked, hating the croaky sound of my voice. I had to stay on my toes and keep moving around so it was harder for them to hit me.

Noah and Reed looked at each other and laughed.

"Hell yes. Good idea."

Reed swung again, and this time he clipped my ear. Hard.

I went down, the cold cobblestones pressing into my hands.

Shit. Get up.

I jumped straight back up to my feet, ignoring the pain in my head.

I tightened my hands into fists and punched Reed in the gut as hard as I possibly could.

He grunted and fell back a few paces, but laughed at the same time.

"Really? Didn't think you had it in you."

Noah stepped up instead of Reed and punched me across the face, making me lose sight for a moment, then I fell onto my back on the cold stones.

Get up. I couldn't fight these guys. I had to run.

I groaned and rolled around on the stones, willing myself to get to my feet. My movements were slower this time. I was having difficulty keeping my vision in focus. But then I saw them laughing and clapping each other on the back.

They thought they had already won.

I groaned again, and staggered a bit more, putting my hand up to my head and acting more disoriented than I really was, so they would think I was really gone.

It worked. They gloated as I wiped at my mouth and moaned.

They turned to give each other a high-five, and I lunged forward and kicked Noah in the nuts. In the same move, I rounded and punched Reed again in the belly. Reed swiped at me as I pivoted and ran past them up the alley, back toward the street. I tripped over the smashed groceries but managed to remain upright, and simply kept on going.

Don't stop. Don't stop.

My breathing was ragged as their footsteps charged behind me.

"Help me!" I began to scream as I approached the alley entrance, appealing to anyone who might hear, or care.

Too late.

One of the men grabbed my hair and pulled me back, hard.

Tears sprung to my eyes as I stared up into the ugly face of my attacker. Reed. His teeth had partially shifted and he glared down at me with death in his eyes.

I wouldn't beg, or plead for my life. Not with him. Not with any of them.

I bared my teeth and growled up at him, even as he yanked again on my hair, tilting my head further back.

Nearby, someone yelled. *Galen*? I hoped it was Galen, and I hoped he would rip these guys apart.

Reed twisted to face whoever was coming.

The movement gave me a slight reprieve and I got my footing, then kicked him hard in a knee. He grunted and pulled my head down. I went with his pull, then twisted out of his grip.

It *was* Galen. He and the guy he had introduced as Darius raced toward us.

Galen reached us first, and punched Reed in the head over and over, until the latter fell to the ground, his nose broken and bleeding all over the place.

Then he came at Noah, who pulled a knife from his belt and held it out in front of himself in a defensive posture. He swiped at Galen, who jumped back and knocked Noah's arm out of the way. Galen brought his arm down on Noah like he was bowling a ball.

Crack. Noah went down, and didn't get up.

Reed went for Galen while his back was turned, but the new guy jumped in and turned to fight at Galen's back, lunging at Reed.

He threw a punch at Reed's face. Reed staggered back.

Justin looked between his buddies and Galen, then turned and ran away, down the alley.

I stumbled sideways, one eye already closed. Pain pushed me to pass out.

I stood my ground as Darius threw another punch at Reed, knocking him out cold. Noah was still on the ground, his face covered in blood. He was either unconscious or dead. I didn't know. And I didn't care at this moment in time.

Now who looks like they got mugged in an alleyway?

I staggered over to my heroes. "Thank you, for saving my life. Again."

Galen twisted to stare at me, his eyes shifted into his wolf.

He took another step closer and pulled me up into his arms, holding me tightly against his body.

"My hero," I whispered, patting his chest.

Galen growled something totally unintelligible, and I began to laugh. Until the darkness took me.

Chapter 16

Galen

I carried Talia back to the bar and considered calling an ambulance. Her face was a mess.

"What do you think?" I asked Darius, as I lay her down on my bed at my apartment above the bar. "Should I take her to the hospital?"

"She's a full wolf shifter, yeah?"

I nodded. "Yeah. As far as I know."

"Then she should heal quickly. You got some ice for her face?"

"Yeah. Down in the bar. Can you get it?" I wasn't leaving her anytime soon. In fact, she was banned from leaving my side ever again.

Darius headed off and I knelt down beside her, brushing her hair off her face. "Every time I leave you alone for ten minutes, something like this happens to you."

Darius came back with multiple small plastic bags of ice and several dry dish cloths. "Great idea," I said, taking the little bags and placing them on her swollen lip and cheek.

"What sort of men do this to a girl?" I said out loud, to no one in particular.

"Cowards," Darius answered, walking over to the corner and sitting on the chair there. "Three against one isn't a fair fight even if you're talking about men, let alone someone as young and small as Talia."

I nodded, because I couldn't say anything else. My wolf had risen up inside me, and it was hard to quiet. I clamped down hard to stop him from ripping through my body and causing a shift here and now.

"They deserve to be hunted down. Those... savages."

Talia groaned, and her eyelids fluttered open. "Who are?"

"You're awake," I said, holding the ice to her jaw. "And I'm talking about those monsters who attacked you. Are you okay? Do you want me to take you to the hospital?"

My father was there, so it would probably save me time, having the two people I was looking after staying in the one place.

"No, I'm fine," Talia said, closing her eyes. "I heal fast."

"I'll head back to the pack for a shower," Darius said. "What time do you want me here for work?"

"Shift starts at eight. People start coming in around nine, and it gets busiest around eleven."

"Be back at eight," Darius said, and then left.

I withdrew my hand from Talia's face so I could stand up and pace. "I can't believe those guys had the nerve to attack you in broad daylight. On neutral territory, too. They could have killed you."

This girl was trouble with a capital T. Her pack wouldn't stop until they had her.

"They intended to," she said softly.

I glanced down at her, and she smiled up at me, one eye swollen shut. "You saving me is beginning to become a habit."

I sighed. "Yeah, well, maybe I'm trying to make up for the mistakes of my past."

"What do you mean?"

I groaned and grabbed the chair from the corner of the room, then dragged it over so I could sit by the side of her bed. "I don't really talk about this..."

She smiled, but didn't say anything, which was exactly what I needed, a moment to think.

I bent forward, resting my elbows on my knees. I couldn't believe I was even contemplating sharing this information, but somehow, the words tumbled out of my mouth. "Her name was Jessie. She was my girlfriend at the time, and we'd been together for a year or so."

"She was a pack member?" Talia asked.

I nodded. "She was. We went to school together. We'd been friends a long time. Then we fell in love..."

I shrugged, the pain of speaking about Jessie getting to me. My heart still hurt.

"What happened?" Talia asked, her voice gentle, soothing.

"She died," I said, though it burnt my throat to admit it.

Talia gasped. "How? What happened?"

"We were attacked." I gulped loudly. "In the woods. I don't remember it very well. Maybe ten people jumped us. All men. I fought them off the best I could. I told her to run."

I shook my head, staring at the wooden floor beneath my feet.

"I was beaten unconscious and when I woke up she was dead, lying a few feet away from me. A head wound so bad she wasn't able to heal."

I swallowed hard, the pain of Jessie's death still haunting me. The failure.

"It wasn't your fault," Talia said, hefting herself up to stare at me.

I lifted my gaze to look at her. "I know that..."

"I don't think you do. You're blaming yourself, when you didn't hurt her. I bet you got really hurt too. How bad were your wounds?"

"Ah..."

It was easier to show her.

I stood up and reached over my head, drawing the shirt off my body.

I pointed at my shoulder. "Knife wound here. Slashed my belly." I indicated the thick white scar dissecting my abs. "Plus twenty stitches in my head."

I put my hand up to the raised flesh cutting across my skull behind my ear. "Broken ribs, nose, eye socket."

I swallowed hard. I shouldn't have survived, and the doctors at the hospital couldn't believe I had.

Talia swung her legs over the side of the bed and stood up, the swelling on her face already noticeably improved.

I raised my hands to cup her cheeks, staring at her injuries. "You're healing already."

She smiled. "Good genes."

She put her hands on my chest, and my heart stopped and then restarted double-time.

"You shouldn't have survived wounds like this, Galen," she whispered, running her fingers along the ugly, white flesh of my belly wound. "Wolf shifters are hard to kill, but we are not immortal, nor death-proof."

"Yeah, ah..." *Think, idiot.* "The doctors didn't believe I'd make it. Especially after I carried Jessie all that way."

Her gaze flicked up to mine. "You what?"

I shrugged. "We were in the middle of nowhere, and I had to get back to the pack. I couldn't carry her body in wolf form, so I just... carried her."

And God, that had hurt. I'd passed out once on the way home, woken up, and kept going. The blood loss had been hardest to deal with. Though the shoulder wound especially had been deep.

Talia trailed her fingers up my chest, bypassing my sensitive nipples and going to my shoulder.

"I can't believe you lived through that. You're... incredible. So strong."

I held her fingers against my shoulder, enjoying the warmth of her. Then I took a step away, breaking contact.

"I'm not incredible. I failed the woman who could have been my mate, my wife. It was my weakness that cost her, her life."

"No," Talia said, strong and sure. "It was the evil of those other men, whoever they were."

I nodded once, reaching for a clean black tank from a drawer next to my bed. "It certainly was."

She wrapped her arms around herself. "I am so grateful for everything you've done for me. But what am I going to do now? I don't want to endanger you, or your pack."

I pulled on the shirt, stretching it over my body and covering myself up once more.

"I want you to stay," I said. "If I thought I could get you out of the state without them catching you, I would. But I don't think it's safe to attempt it yet."

Talia nodded, then sighed. "Yeah, you're probably right."

I glanced toward the door to the bedroom. "Look. I need to get the bar ready for the night. I won't leave, don't worry. I'll get some food delivered, and it's gonna be loud, but hopefully you can get some rest."

She bit her lip and climbed back onto the bed. "Thanks."

I went out of the bedroom and shut the door that connected the stairs from the apartment down to the bar. I'd get her some food, work all night, and make sure no one came near her.

Then I'd sleep on the couch and hopefully get a good night's sleep myself.

It was beginning to niggle at me that I'd shared so much of myself with a girl I'd only known a few days. And for most of those days, I'd considered her a bargaining tool.

I had to reconsider my whole position on Talia, and how I was going to use the information she gave me to do as my father had asked, and avenge our pack.

TALIA

I closed my eyes and listened to the intense beat of the music rising up from below. My belly was full, thanks to Galen, and I was warm and dry.

Also, thanks to him, I was lying in a comfortable, clean bed, safe from the pack that hunted me.

I still couldn't believe I'd almost died today. Twice.

Galen had been my knight in shining armor. Or fur, in our case.

He was so much stronger, and more truly Alpha, than any man I'd ever known. I couldn't even begin to compare him with Maddox. There was nothing Alpha in Maddox—I could see that now. When it came to Galen, not only was he huge, and strong, and powerful, he was thoughtful. Understanding. Empathetic.

When he told me about his girlfriend dying in a brutal attack that almost killed them both, my heart had broken for him. He must have blamed himself for such a long time after; and it seemed to me like he still did.

Survivor guilt must have been the absolute worst. It was similar in some ways to my father.

I turned onto my side. The sounds of the music in the club beneath me should have kept me awake. Instead, I found the constant noise soothing. I knew Galen was down there, watching out for me.

I trusted him. He wanted me to be a part of his pack, and he'd proven twice now that he was willing to kill to save me.

Maddox had never done such a thing. If anything, in truth, he'd thrown me out. His father had wanted me gone, and despite him being my fated mate, he hadn't stood up for me.

What did that say about our relationship? About Maddox himself?

I moaned softly, burying my head in the pillow. My head ached, but thanks to the medication Galen had given me after dinner, I was beginning to drift off.

Sleep tugged at me, pulling me down into the darkness.

My body was sore, and my heart had been broken. But I was still here, and I was still fighting for my life. And now I had a tiny bit of hope for the future, where earlier, I had nothing.

Yesterday, I hadn't been so sure I would fight if it came down to it, but today proved to me that I would and could.

Despite losing everything, I desperately wanted to live. To see where the rest of my life's journey would take me.

And at the moment, my journey had led to Galen.

To his pack, with his scars, and his strength.

There were a lot worse places to be, and that included my old pack grounds.

Chapter 17

Galen

Sleeping on my couch in the apartment was almost worse than sleeping on the old sofa in the cabin. When the sun rose, I woke up and rolled off the couch, falling to the ground with a thud.

From the bed, Talia moaned softly, but didn't wake. She was probably still a little doped up on pain medication.

I got to my feet and walked over to her, staring down at her glorious red and gold hair, and her beautiful face, as she rested peacefully on one of my pillows.

She was looking so much healthier this morning. Most of the bruising and swelling was gone, leaving only remnants of the blood-smeared battle she'd waged yesterday.

She couldn't fight, that was obvious. But she'd tried, and that said something for a female up against three males.

I was proud of her. Even though she wasn't mine to be proud of.

Well, she was officially a member of my pack now, so I supposed that I was allowed to be, at least a little. She could use some fighting lessons, though.

I crept into the small kitchen and made eggs for breakfast, checking my cell phone for any messages from my Betas.

I'd told them I would bring Talia back to the pack this morning for her own safety and introduce her to some of the women. Then, while she was occupied, and safe, I'd hunt with some of the men.

I needed it. My nerves were stretched tight and I had to get out for a run.

I still couldn't believe that I'd told Talia about Jessie. I didn't talk to anyone about her, not even my dad. It was a gruesome and dark part of my past that I never liked to look back on, let alone speak about.

But Talia's very presence made me want to open up and talk to her. I didn't know how she did it, or what had possessed me to show her all my scars. But I had. Literally and figuratively.

"Good morning," came her small voice from behind me.

I turned around, frying pan in hand. "Hey. You want some breakfast?"

She nodded and rubbed her eyes like a sleepy kid.

But there was nothing childish about the miles of leg that showed beneath the oversized sweater she'd worn to bed last night.

Her thighs were creamy and smooth, and made me want to toss breakfast in the sink, throw her over my shoulder, and take her back to bed.

I coughed to clear my throat. "Come sit down."

I shoved off the papers and crap that had accumulated on my dining room table and put a couple of plates down.

Talia sat, and I served her, the softness of the aura that surrounded her making me sigh.

"Eat up. I've got juice, and coffee if you want?"

"Thanks. This is great," she said, grabbing a fork and beginning to eat the scramble I'd made for her.

It had been so long since I'd had a woman stay in my bed. Too long to count, actually. I was a little rough on the whole breakfast-with-another-person thing.

"We'll go back to the pack this morning. It's safer there for you," I said, picking up my plate and sitting down next to her to eat.

"That sounds great." She ate a few more forkfuls, then asked, "Where will I stay? At the log cabin again?"

I laughed. "No, you're not my prisoner, and I don't like the idea of you being trapped in a house."

She grinned at me. "You didn't seem to mind a couple of days ago."

I shrugged. "A lot has changed in two days."

"Yes, it has." She stared at me, her eyes wide and vulnerable pools that I wanted to dive right into.

I broke the eye contact, scooped up the last of my eggs, and went to the sink to wash up.

This girl wasn't good for me. I felt as young and vulnerable as an eighteen-year-old with his first crush. It was unsettling.

"You wanna get changed, and we'll go right away?"

She stood up and brought her plate over to me. "Yeah. Of course. Thank you so much."

I grimaced out a smile and started the dishes so she'd walk away. I was going to put her in Dad's house, but maybe I should shove her down the back of the pack with some of the other women her age.

But what if her pack came to grab her? And hurt some of our females?

Nope. That wasn't happening. There was only one place she would be safe, and that was right beside me.

Talia walked back out of the bedroom a few minutes later in a pair of black leggings and a gray t-shirt. "All ready."

"Great," I said, though my mouth was dry. "Give me five minutes and we'll go."

I went and changed quickly, my hands shaking while I did. I was filled with nervous adrenaline. Damn, I really needed that run.

I grabbed the keys, locked up, and escorted my new pack member to my truck.

"Jump in and buckle your seat belt," I told her, hopping in my side. "I still can't believe the nerve of your old pack. They attack us out of nowhere. Then they try to take you down in the middle of town, even though town is considered neutral."

I turned the key in the engine and we started driving along the road.

"Yeah, I reminded them of the neutrality when they attacked. But they just said that as long as they didn't shift, they could attack me and everyone would think I'd been mugged and murdered. Just another dead girl in an alleyway."

She shivered, and then stared out the window, and although I couldn't see her face, I could hear the pain in her voice.

"I'm sorry this happened to you."

She nodded, but didn't look at me. I hadn't asked why she'd been kicked out of her pack, and I wasn't sure she'd tell me if I asked.

It seemed deeply personal.

For a fated mate to reject her, something terrible must have happened. Had Talia been caught with another guy? Or had Maddox himself fallen for another?

Or was it something completely unrelated to their relationship? The timing seemed too coincidental, that she'd been thrown out of the pack the day after the fight.

But I didn't ask.

She'd tell me in her own time, or it would all come out soon enough. Secrets and lies tended to be unearthed, even when people wanted them buried.

"We're almost there," I said as we passed the large iron gates that led onto my pack grounds. "I'll set you up in a bedroom at my dad's house, then you can rest and relax. How are you feeling today?"

She sighed and glanced over at me. "A bit heart broken, but hey… I'll live. Hopefully."

I pulled over in front of my dad's place and looked straight at her. "You're safe here. I promise. As long as I've got breath in my body, I'll fight for you."

She trembled as though my vow had physically affected her.

I reached out and squeezed her hand, wanting the connection, for some unfathomable reason.

She glanced down at my hand and smiled. "Thank you, Galen."

I nodded, then pulled my hand away, my palm tingling from the contact. "Great. Let's go."

I settled Talia into my dad's place.

Then I called Darius, who'd been a real asset in the bar last night and in the alleyway fight yesterday. I was beginning to trust him, even after this short time, and at least I knew he could hold his ground. "Come over to my dad's place and stay outside until I get back. Have a smoke, whatever. Just keep an eye on her and don't leave her alone."

"Yeah, not a problem."

Within five minutes, he was on my doorstep.

"I won't be long," I told him. "I'll be back as soon as I can."

Markus waved at me from the front step of his place, and I jogged after him. My shifter was aching for a run.

"Let's go, man. What are we looking for today? Rabbits? Foxes?"

Markus shrugged. "Whatever. Food is food, right?"

I nodded. I wasn't hungry, and I never ate a live animal while in wolf form. But it was good for the pack to bring home game, and good for the local pest problem, too.

Not to mention the fact that us guys got to run and fight, and kill stuff.

It was basic, but our wolves needed it.

I was gone long enough to fulfil that need in me, but as soon as I started to feel anxious about being away from Talia, I turned tail and raced home.

When I got there, Darius was nowhere to be seen.

"Hello?" I called out, and Mary-Anne, one of my dad's neighbors, popped her head over the fence.

"Galen!" she said, smiling at me.

"Have you seen Darius or Talia?" I asked her, worry making my skin itch.

"The new Beta and the girl?" she asked. "Yeah. They said Talia needed to get something from her car, and you'd left it in town."

"Shit. I did."

We'd driven it in yesterday, and she'd been too unwell to drive it back.

I hated having to change the plan all the time, but the goal posts kept shifting and the end game was still unknown.

"Thanks, Mary-Anne."

"They said they wouldn't be long."

I grimaced out a smile and headed into the house for clothes. I'd begun to trust Darius, but not one hundred percent yet. I didn't know him well enough to believe that Talia would be fine with him outside of these pack grounds.

And I certainly didn't trust Talia's pack not to attack her again if they had the chance. I'd been there to save her the past two times, and I needed to make sure I was there again.

I threw on some clothes, grabbed the keys, and jumped in my dad's truck, since they'd taken mine to the bar.

My teeth were clenched tight as I pulled onto the main road and headed back into town.

They were probably fine. I would see them driving on the other side of the street and they'd call me a fool for worrying.

But I didn't turn back.

I *was* a fool. This girl wasn't mine. I barely knew her. And yet, I was determined to keep her safe.

My truck was still parked out in front of the bar. The hairs on the back of my neck stood on end.

Where the hell were they?

I barged into the bar. "Talia? Darius?"

"Just out the back!" Talia called.

My heart leapt in my chest and tension eased from my body.

I unclenched my fists and strode through the bar, grabbing a beer from the fridge on my way through. My nerves were shot.

"You should have waited for me..." I started to say as I walked out the back door, then caught sight of Talia.

She was standing by her dad's old car, staring off into the distance.

"Talia!"

She didn't respond.

"Hey! Talia!" I called again, walking toward her. I waved my hand in front of her face.

She looked frozen in place, and her eyes were glazed over. What the hell was this? It looked like someone had cast a spell over her. So, where was the witch who was working the magic?

And where the hell was Darius?

I caught something in the reflection of Talia's eyes and twisted, fast. *Fucking hell.* It was a demon. They were so rare I'd never actually seen one, only heard of them, but there was no mistaking what it was.

It stood like a man, but it had no face. No features, no clothes. It was a blackened shadow with flames for eyes.

"Get out of here!" I growled at it, stepping in front of Talia to block the demon's view.

It lifted its hand, as though anxious for the woman behind me. *That's weird.* My father had told me of demons' alluring qualities, and I could see from the way Talia continued to stare in its direction that it was calling her. Just like a siren's call.

Town rules be damned. I let the shift rip through me, and my black wolf leapt forth. I planted my feet on the concrete in front of Talia and bared my teeth at the demon.

It flared, the brightness of its flames burning hotter. Dark magic. These things were fucking evil. And it had to be stopped from getting whatever it wanted to acquire from Talia.

I growled, but the demon didn't move. These things were deadly.

I launched forward, running straight at it.

Its arms dropped, and then it disappeared from view as it ran down the street. I stopped short at the corner of the building and shifted back to human before anyone in town saw me.

I was naked now, and panting hard.

I stuck my head around the corner, but the demon was gone.

I shook myself. "What the hell was that?"

I turned and jogged back to Talia, my heart thumping in my chest.

She shivered, then dragged her gaze up to my eyes. "You're naked. What happened?"

"A fucking demon just turned up and attempted to lure you away. Don't you remember anything?"

Her mouth dropped open. "A demon? Are you insane?"

I growled in frustration.

Darius called through from the bar. "Hey, Talia. You still here? We've gotta get going. Galen—" He stepped through the back door and stopped dead. "Is already here."

"Hell yeah, I'm here. I told you to watch her. Keep her safe. Do you think that meant bringing her here, where she almost died, and then leaving her alone?"

Talia put her hand on my arm, drawing my attention. "It's my fault, Galen. I'm sorry. I didn't know how long you'd be and I thought getting my dad's car and parking it where I'm going to be living was smarter."

I scratched my head and took a long deep breath. "Let's just get going. You both get back in your prospective cars, and head off. I'll be two minutes behind you. I've gotta go grab some more clothes."

I stormed into the bar and ran up the stairs. The jeans I'd just ripped to shreds in the unexpected shift had been my favorite pair.

I tugged on sweatpants and a t-shirt, irritated and angry. What the hell was a demon doing in town? And what did it want with Talia?

Maybe time would tell, but one thing was for sure. Once we got back to the pack, I wasn't letting the woman out of my sight again, even if it meant sleeping in the same room as her and making her come on runs and patrols with me.

I couldn't trust anyone else to look after her, and after failing to protect Jessie, I wasn't losing Talia, too.

The human part of me knew that she wasn't mine to protect. But the wolf part wanted her claimed, and whilst I couldn't do that, I would do the next best thing. I would protect her as if she was mine.

To be continued... in book 2.

Wolf of Blood.

Printed in Great Britain
by Amazon